The Art
of
Contraception

Susie Wild is a writer, journalist and editor based in south Wales. She was born in 1979, and her words have appeared all over the shop, including *Nu: fiction & stuff*, *Mslexia*, *New Welsh Review*, *Planet*, *The Big Issue*, the BBC, *Clash Magazine* and *The Guardian*. A Goldsmiths graduate, if you put letters after her name they would spell 'BAMAMA'; she would rather 'banana' so does not use them. She regularly performs her poetry in dives and dance halls. *The Art of Contraception* is her first book.

The Art
of
Contraception

Susie Wild

PARTHIAN

Parthian
The Old Surgery
Napier Street
Cardigan
SA43 1ED

First published in 2010
© Susie Wild 2010
All Rights Reserved
ISBN 978-1-906998-03-5

Editor: Lucy Llewellyn
Cover design by Tim Albin www.droplet.co.uk
Inner design & typesetting by Lucy Llewellyn
Printed by Gwasg Gomer, Llandysul

Published with the financial support of the Welsh Books Council.

For your FREE eBook follow these simple steps:
1) find the password: 3rd word on page 11
2) log on to www.parthianbooks.com
3) add 'The Art of Contraception eBook' to your shopping cart
4) add the password when prompted
5) select 'Free order only' option at the checkout
You will then receive an email with a link to your free eBook

British Library Cataloguing in Publication Data
A cataloguing record for this book is available from the British Library.

Lyrics by My Brightest Diamond used with kind permission from
Asthmatic Kitty Records, and from the *Bugsy Malone* film from Polydor.

For my friends, with thanks

CONTENTS

Aquatic Life   1

Diving Lessons   9

Pocillovy   17

Paying for Sex   25

Pica   33

Sauce   43

Big on Japan   51

Waxing, Waning   57

Flap, Flap   65

Dreams, Inconsistent Angel Things   71

Stung   85

Arrivals, a novella   95

'Love is the answer – but while you're waiting for the answer sex raises some pretty good questions.'

Woody Allen

Unfortunate Coincidence

By the time you swear you're his,
Shivering and sighing,
And he vows his passion is
Infinite, undying –
Lady, make a note of this:
One of you is lying.

Dorothy Parker

Aquatic Life

Instead of going abroad, Rob liked to take his holidays in the bath. He spent his time off splashing around like a channel-crossing swimmer, or with his scuba-masked face under the surface, watching plastic fish bop around him in the murky shallows. He'd sip cocktails perched on the side of the tub with his feet dangling into the water as if at the side of a swimming pool in the Med, and blast samba tunes from a stereo in his studio flat bedroom-slash-lounge, imagining bikini-clad ladies swaying their bronzed hips in time to a live band.

As night fell the aquatic man would pull himself out of the draining water and lay his beach towel on top of his sand coloured duvet, dozing and drying out under the bright lights of his sunbed, attempting to get a plausible tan for his post-holiday cigarette-break stories about Goa or Bangkok or The Gambia. His laptop laid open on the relevant travel pages; he would try to learn names and facts in the eerie blue glow. He'd wow them with the things he'd seen, reciting practised conversations and fascinating teaser anecdotes.

'I went to the Canary Islands last week – lovely they was. Their second biggest export is pumice stone, I found that *very* interesting.' Or: 'No, see, a little known fact is that the best time to visit Goa is monsoon season. I didn't even mind the rain, although swimming in the sea was out of the question.'

He would spend hours working on his most convincing, animated voice, just like the one he'd hear Sylvie use when spilling her secrets to him.

Upon his shower curtain two tall palm trees climbed high into the glossy turquoise sky, towering above his head. The white tiles of the surround were plastered in a collage of pictures with the contrast turned up; all ripped from holiday brochures and newspaper travel supplements. Rope bridges through lush jungles, brightly coloured drinks served in coconut shells with umbrellas, dolphins curling through ocean waters and lines of curvaceous youngsters wearing nothing but smiles and grass skirts.

The girls in the pictures did not look like Sylvie, but that is who he dreamed he was spending his trips with. He would picture her smooth, translucent surfaces turning pink under the hot sun. Rob looked more like a beached sea lion; his white folds of skin crumpled and creased with new wrinkles, and fell heavily around him in the tub. He snored in mews and roars which caused the neighbours to strain with glasses at the vibrating walls, wondering at his sexual practices.

The holidays of Rob's mind were – he was sure – more entertaining and exotic than anything that would happen if he were actually away on wild tropical islands, or white-walled Costa del Sol resorts. Certainly more entertaining than his days pushing papers in the concrete council offices of his normal nine-to-five. But not as entertaining as the images that Sylvie had conjured up in the dark basement of walled files for him. The wide and wonderful world that she was going to travel... just as soon as she left school.

Sylvie's dad worked upstairs. She used to come to meet him from work on Wednesdays after school, and after her piano lesson on a leafy street just around the corner, so that she could get a lift to their clean, suburban home. The first time Rob saw her he had jumped. Sort of. She had been skulked in a ball on the steps to the basement fire exit, a feral creature. After the initial shock he had seen that she wasn't an animal at all but a girl – all delicate, petite features and big, nicotine-laced exhales that had dwarfed her even more. They had fallen into the easy conversations that all smokers can, aided by the air of the illicit. He had ignored her school uniform and she had ignored his make-it-a-large-one size.

Rob had liked Sylvie, and he had found this strange because he didn't generally like many people. Anyone, in fact. Not even his mother. But then who would like a mother who drank her own weight in Lambrini and ran off with the mobile hairdresser? Especially a mother who only got as far as opening a blue-rinse salon two streets away and never visited, although Rob's dad could often be found there making a scene. Sylvie was different. She talked to Rob for ages and about every little thing that popped into her head from how she'd quite like to look like Amy Winehouse, before the major tumble from grace, to why chickpeas were called chickpeas when they didn't contain any meat. Her mother was one of those upper middle-class eco types who'd die if she saw Sylvie wolfing down a McDonald's, which meant she could have died more than 300 times over. And when Rob spoke, telling Sylvie his stored facts and rehearsed holiday tales, the tinkle of her laugh didn't seem to jibe like others' previously had.

At school Rob hadn't had any human friends. He'd quite liked the croaky toad in the pond at St Fagin's Primary, and the biology teacher at sixth form, because she let him eat his lunch in the labs while reading illustrated science books about

3

aquatic life. There he had washed away his loneliness with watery facts: *sea lions do not mate for life; young male Steller's sea lions, known as bachelors, remain isolated until they are large enough to compete with mature adult males for a territory.* Unlike Rob's dad.

Sylvie liked Rob because he let her talk – with her friends she couldn't get a word in, well, rarely, and her parents would hate to know what she thought about all day long. It was hardly rocket science: boys, rock music, smoking, and escaping from said parents and their crappy town. As soon as she could. On a jet plane.

Sat in his bathtub Rob was sweating. His heating was turned up to 11 – tropical – while a desk fan perched on the windowsill, pointing its meagre breeze at the quickly cooling bathwater to create gentle waves, but failing to produce his much-desired surf and spray. No relief. His thoughts were turning more feverish with the rising temperatures. He could feel his temper bubbling, a kettle about to boil. A phrase caught like a stuck record in the soundtrack of his torrid mind – *I haven't done anything wrong.*

It was Bethan who had discovered the pictures. For some unfathomable reason she had been sent down to the basement to find a document. Rob had been on one of his many sneaky fag breaks, and not around to consult, and so this irritable, incompetent busybody had tried to find it herself; nosing about and causing all sorts of chaos that would have taken Rob weeks to sort out again. Would have. If the stupid fool hadn't unearthed his collage of ripped pictures, some with the contrast turned up, some not, but all featuring a silvery-skinned girl smiling. The same young girl, in each and every raggedy-edged one. Rob had kept it in the top drawer of his desk to bring comfort during the dull, dark days. He remembered the afternoon they were taken. She'd turned up brandishing a digital camera, all shiny and new, a crooked smile on her lunar face inviting him to try it out. She'd said that she was no good with gadgets, and she pulled the same Am-I-Bothered pose in each shot. Had wanted some new profile pictures for her Facehack or BimBo or whatever it was called. And perhaps for someone else; a scribbled e-mail address on a fag packet. Her boyfriend. Rob hadn't sent them there though; he'd pretended there must be a problem with his bandwidth; or perhaps new IT restrictions at work. His tales stretched to anything but the truth: his jealousy.

Rob had been sent home early on the day of Bethan's meddling, had been told that some routine building work had been scheduled in, and that he needn't come back to work until Monday. Oblivious to the truth he had treated it like another holiday: turned up the heating, filled the bath, dug out his Bermuda shorts; happily splashy-splashy. But then, on Monday, he was called into the office and told that perhaps he might like to take a longer holiday from work; that perhaps, under the circumstances, that might be appropriate. That he wasn't being accused of anything; he wasn't being sacked. Rob found that he didn't really want another holiday. Not one alone, at any rate.

He had tried to find the enjoyment he used to gain so easily goofing around in the bathtub... but he couldn't conjure up Sylvie's moon-face, round and beaming above her tiny body. He hadn't been allowed to collect any of his things from the basement, to seek one last glance at his collection of photos. To tamper with what was now referred to as 'The Evidence'.

Huffing and puffing, Rob hauled himself out of the tub, and decided to change tack. He typed 'Eskimo Music' into the internet search engine box on his tool bar, before clicking, once, twice, and three times to get the first new tracks to play. He turned the volume up, and drained the bath. Next he poured in cold water and opened all three windows in his compact living space. He pulled open the fridge and began to chip away at the ice from the freezer compartment, sprinkling his goods into the bath tub like tiny splinters of iceberg. He needed to cool down, to gain some clarity of thinking.

Rob wasn't one to run away from trouble. He didn't have such impulses in him. He couldn't jump that fast, physically or mentally. He knew that he should try and remember the things that Sylvie had said. About her boyfriend. The 'Boyfriend This' and 'Boyfriend That' stuff. But the thing was he hadn't listened to those bits. Not properly. He'd replaced the boyfriend's name with his own, or just zoned out completely; imagining what he would do if she were his girlfriend. Though it turned out that he wasn't entirely sure; he'd never actually had one. He figured it involved going places together, and perhaps, once in a while, holding hands. He would have liked to hold her hand.

Sylvie's dad wanted somebody to blame for his daughter's recent spat of bad behaviour. All the smoking and shagging around and skipping school. The getting pregnant and showing. It being obvious to anyone who looked, and right before her GCSEs, with the council-bloody-elections in just a few weeks. He knew that his daughter had her mother's brains, but he'd hoped she may have taken on some of his sense. Instead of running around town with that Aaron Pryce. Luckily for him there was a scapegoat – a scape-whale – in the Supersize-Me form of Rob Evans. He'd been seen with her on many an occasion, by the basement fire escape, and, even better, Sylvie's dad's secretary Bethan had discovered the crushed-heart collage of photos, and then planted some more unsavoury ones into the collection. As he'd instructed. There'd be a local media to-do, once he'd made the right phone calls; the town paper loved a good paedo story. They would probably print Rob's name and address shamelessly, before any court case even needed to happen, leaving Sylvie's dad's election campaign bacon saved. It was child's play.

Rob was halfway through running himself a cold bath when the water suddenly stopped, leaving the tap spluttering and then screeching; a high-pitched wail. He turned the tap off and the noise eased. He turned the tap on again and the noise returned, louder, but no water came. He tried the hot tap. Nothing. He could hear the boiler struggling, the thud and clatter of low pressure in the pipes. Wearily standing up, both feet partially submerged by H_2O, he began hauling his fleshy paws at the taps, frustrated. He realised that he would never be able to go on holiday with Sylvie now, and not only because he was absolutely petrified of flying.

He swiped at the high contrast collage of dream holidays on the tiles, and they dropped to the bottom of the tub, shrinking and shrivelling all around him. He emitted a low, strangled mew and angrily kicked the side of the bath, and as he did so the desk fan, still twirling, flew off its precarious perch and knocked Rob into the tub, flipping him flat onto his back like a hooked fish, twitching in the shallow puddles of a boat deck, once, twice, and then dead.

Diving Lessons

Archie is *not* listening to his girlfriend. He is looking at her but past her, beyond the rain-stained glass of the waterside chain bar with its exhibits of framed prints, crap beer and an even crapper clientele. He's looking at the girl sat outside the art gallery opposite. She is sat stock still – frozen – her rigid form adopting a diving position, arms arced, knees drawn up to her chin. Her long bedraggled hair clings flat to her face in strands, stuck by the downpour. Archie can't read her expression, nor tell if that man on the bench to her right is her man, or simply another stranger. Archie's girlfriend gestures as she talks, oblivious, liquid splashing from her wine glass and hitting him like spit.

John, however, *is* listening to *his* girlfriend, although she complains that he isn't. He is listening and watching from a safe distance, sat upon a damp bench, as she comes dangerously close to falling into the dirty harbourside water. She is ranting at him about his recent behaviour. She is drunk. She teeters. She raises her arms as if to dive. She is crying. Big tears pour from even bigger eyes. He thinks she looks beautiful all the same. Crazy and beautiful, and he doesn't know how to say sorry. He doesn't know how to make things better, how to right his wrongs, or even how wrong he has actually been, but he is hoping that he will come up with something soon. He hopes this because he cannot swim.

Lottie is sat on a wet slab of stone. Her legs are dangling over the water now, and her thin arced arms are somehow graceful. She is wondering what it would be like to be swimming, deep down below the surface, away from all that Friday night noise that explodes in the streets and in her head – the chatter and clatter; smashing times, smashing glasses and smashed lives. She is hoping for dark and silence, for calm. She has not been acting with silence or calm. Irately punch-drunk – she has been shouting. She has been yelling and contradicting herself. She has been wronged, and she is wrong, but she wants it to stop. She doesn't know how to find her way back. She can only stare at the surface of the water and think of its depths. Wait for her temper to ebb. Hope for intervention.

In the bar, Archie's girlfriend can see a print on the wall behind her man's head. It is by Roy Lichtenstein; she can't pronounce his name. It is big. A huge cartoon. She thinks it is the sort of thing her brother might like, except that you can't see the girl's tits. In the print a tearful woman with a blue bob is drowning. A cartoon speech bubble floats from her mouth: 'I don't care! I'd rather sink – than call Brad for help!' Archie's girlfriend doesn't read the speech bubble, or really take in the scene, she neither knows nor cares about art, but she does like the girl's haircut. It looks smart and sophisticated; classy. She wonders if it would suit her. She asks Archie. He replies by sipping his flat beer, and then pulling a face. She takes that as a no.

Archie knows what it is like to swim below the surface. He does it every day. He thinks back to a time in the village, when he was a boy. A hand holding his head underwater to the count of '1, 2, 3...' A humid day. Of coming up ghoul-faced, skinny-ribbed and gasping to peals of laughter from his spiteful peers. Those same peers, now left behind, would cower at his bulk today. Archie is pulled back to the here and now by his girlfriend slamming down her empty glass.

'You're not listening to me *Arch-eey*.' The words tilt, the start of a slur. She pouts.

'Same again?' he asks blankly. He can't be bothered with another fight, not tonight.

She nods, childlike, and mouths a kiss at his retreating form.

John is watching Lottie's back as her breathing slows and settles; her stiff body relaxing, but still on the edge. He searches for the right words. They are both hurting. They have both lost. After what happened at the hospital it is too soon to be out, and yet too soon not to be drunk. He vows to take swimming lessons, or to move them both to the middle of the country, away from rivers, lakes and deep puddles, a house without baths. He does not want to lose her. He thinks at least they can, when they want to, when the time is right, at least they know that they can make a baby. They could make four. He knows these are not the right words.

Lottie's thoughts are drifting; her eyes closed. She is back in the chill of the hospital ward. From the window she can see the smiling curve of Swansea Bay. See people in shorts and tees racing around the sports fields across the way, the sun beating down as the blood gushes from between her legs and the cramps rise and subside to dull aches, rise and subside, like the tide lapping upon the shore, and the tears pouring down her cheeks. Nobody else in the room appears to be crying, or aching. An old woman sleeps in the bed across the way, a fig in blankets. Lottie doesn't know why the silver-haired one is there; she is too old to conceive, perhaps too old even to breathe. In contrast a cherry-popped pubescent paces the room, dressed and ready to go. In the adjacent bed another woman, about Lottie's age, tells her little boy that she loves him, and that his tea is by the microwave. 'Mummy will be home soon,' she coos into her mobile phone. Lottie wants to call John, but she doesn't. She lies still, she plays dead.

John is remembering the hospital too. Lottie's brave face in the car, the awkward nervous tics, the gasped tears. The inappropriate lust as they waited, having arrived too early. The kind that swells at funerals, that fills voids, that allows the bereaved to feel something, anything. John felt lost. He willed the process over, wanted his life back on track again, the fear finished with. The nurse was frosty as he dropped Lottie off at the ward. Told him he could pick the patient up this evening, and that he was not allowed to stay. 'Six hours, perhaps more,' and yet he was not permitted to go to the pub and drink because he had to drive Lottie home later. Too much time to think.

Archie wanted a child – he wasn't getting any younger – but his much younger girlfriend didn't. 'Not yet,' she'd whisper, 'not yet' and then she'd do something suitably rude to try and ensure that the subject was forgotten, although it wasn't. He understood; he had been the same once. He had paid out at the private abortion clinic more than once before. Later he had ignored the calls. He would be forty next week. He could feel the pull of mortality, his body kept finding new ways not to do what he wanted it to. He didn't want his offspring's lasting memories of him to be related to age. He didn't want them to see him as too old when they were only children, but it was inevitable.

Archie's girlfriend was still talking at him, something about a haircut he wouldn't be sticking around to see. He couldn't imagine growing old with her. The one person he could imagine getting silly and senile with, grey and creaking, was long gone. Three kids with the next bloke that came along, but he couldn't be bitter. She had asked Archie first, pleaded, and he had laughed in her face. He couldn't blame her for moving on. Other than that, maturing, growing old, hadn't really been on his mind. Why would it be when he was getting an eyeful of thong, a handful of cheek? Why did people have to love people anyway? He didn't love his girlfriend, he barely liked her, but one way or another Archie wasn't quite ready to leave, to be alone. 'Not yet,' he thought.

John's mum was afraid of the water. For no reason other than that she was. Just as his mate Ben's golden retriever ran barking from the choppy waves on the shore, scared of the sea, so too did his mother run away from the coastal village she grew up in, seeking sanctuary further inland. She instilled this feeling within John as he grew, a steeping infusion of fear. He had sick notes for mandatory school swimming lessons. He never learnt to breast stroke, to front crawl, to doggy paddle even. It hadn't ever really struck him as a problem. He had grown up in a concrete city. It was only recently that he had moved nearer water, for Lottie. She needed to be near the sea, she said, to feel sane, to feel whole. John stared at her back, and realised he had never felt as scared as he did now. *Calming thoughts*, he instructed himself, *breathe deeply*.

He sought out a show reel of Polaroid niceness; sun-bright memories. 'Dive in!' That is what Lottie had said when they met. 'Dive in, John. Jump. This is real.' They were standing in the kitchen at a friend's party. She had squeezed his hand and smiled. He had kissed her.

Archie's girlfriend still liked to party, a stereotypical twenties weekender. Crap job, crap life, but who cares, doesn't matter, not bothered. A few lines of coke would sort it. Some dancing, some recovering, some vomiting and back to nine to five work, innit? The self-inflicted suffering cushioned the daily mundanity. The weekday evenings were spent staring at mindless TV in the countdown until Friday, or, more recently Thursday. Besides, she didn't want the stretch marks, or any of the other horrible effects motherhood had on a woman's looks. She'd seen it happen to her sister. It was revolting; gross. She was a material girl, not maternal – she'd thought Archie knew that. She looks over at him, a long, hard stare. He has said even less than usual tonight. He definitely wasn't listening to her. Or looking at her. Her eyes narrow as she turns around and tries to work out what he's looking at. She doesn't notice the diving girl opposite, but the wine in her veins invokes her to see something in nothing. A brunette in the harbourside beer garden stubs her cigarette out with the stiletto heel of her boots, smiles at something her friend says. Archie's girlfriend thinks she spies an adulterous glint in his eyes, some unspoken promise to the brunette spelled out in the reciprocal upward curving of his lips. She doesn't like what she thinks she sees.

Lottie comes to as if she has been sleeping, breaking from her trance to see the water sway invitingly below her. She shakes out her stiff, arced arms and rubs at her damp, drowsy eyes.

She thinks for a moment, regains bearings. Glances to her right and sees John looking back at her, all boyish and worried; a tug on her heart strings. It was a look that had won her over, love at second sight. Lottie turns away, sobers a tad, and the abdominal ache resurfaces, along with the faint taste of bile. Silent tears. She turns to John again and offers a wilted half-smile, an apology of sorts, before turning her attention back to the rippling surface below, the hidden depths. She leans forward and hopes for calm, for silence beneath the surface.

Splash!

Liquid showers the scene. Heads turn, necks crane.

Archie's girlfriend has thrown a drink over him, a slap in the face for suspected infidelities. As he blinks in disbelief he catches the scorn in her eyes, the indignant smile that creeps across her cheeks. Through the syrupy veil of sweet white wine he sees the man from the bench pulling the diving girl up from her perch, and close to him, safely inland. Archie seems to find the momentum to get to his feet. He steps through the bar's glass patio doors and into the drizzle. Sparking up a cigarette, he leans upon the safety rail that protects the drunk from their drunken urges, the despair. The couple still hold their embrace, as if they have come up for air, gasping for one another, and as Archie watches he pulls hard on his nicotine stick, feels the rain soaking through his open jacket, his black shirt. It washes away the wine from his freckled skin. He sticks out his tongue to catch raindrops, and feels a thirst long forgotten, a thirst for life.

Pocillovy

NB: *POCILLOVY* / Collecting egg cups. A word of narrow focus and specialist appeal, this is rare enough that no dictionary has yet opened its pages to admit it.

The egg cup had been missing for hours, days even. Its vanishing act had left the air in the new flat unsettled – disrupted by a flurry of activity as both occupiers rechecked the cupboards, the window ledges, and the remainder of unpacked boxes hidden under the bed. They recalled the last time they had seen it. There had been laughter and music and wine. There had been dancing, the shallow sound sneaking through the laptop's inbuilt speakers over the whirr of its engine; the man's samba moves causing the ceiling in the flat below to creak. The egg cup had sat, white and squat and strangely proud, on the dining table, dwarfed by the wooden pepper grinder beside it, the salt crystals held in its concave centre shimmering in the crooked candlelight. The woman had seasoned her meal, two small pinches scattered like ashes over her plate.

They were a couple in love and in the early years of still discovering. More so with each well-lubricated conversation and every post-coital pillow rambling; with each opened and emptied box hauled from storage at places neither called home – discarded hobbies and haircuts, dead pets and relationships.

The half-lives led before this shared one. After years of communal living she now had a place to call home. Alice and Tim. Left alone at last in their first floor flat; their compact castle above the city. So far, so fairy tale.

Alice thought that finding the egg cup was essential to the health and survival of her relationship. Just as much as keeping the windowsill plants alive – the small heart-shaped cacti picked up on impulse in IKEA, and two flowering pots of pink and white offloaded from Tim's parents. She believed in superstitions, her own little rituals. She was a human Magic 8 Ball, since she was a little girl; a magic fairy, a sorcerer. *If I roll a six, Daddy will bring us chips for tea. If I wear my hair in plaits, Richie will ask me to the cinema. If I'm nice to Mum for a whole day, I will get an A in chemistry. If the plants don't wilt, shrivel and die neither will our love. If he likes his meal, Tim will not leave. If I find the egg cup, he will come home.*

Her belly growling for breakfast, Alice opened a kitchen cupboard. Inside, the other white egg cup looked bereft, besides the two blue bowls, the pairs of large and small plates, the his-and-hers peanut butter. Tim was not in the flat. He was often not in the flat. From Monday to Friday there was the office, which was not in the flat. Then he was pretty likely to be at the after-work drinks, and the drinks after that... This time was different. A business trip away. Four long days and three nights alone and Alice had a fever. When she stepped outside the flat as night fell, the bright Christmas lights made her feel giddy, she hallucinated; she would see Tim's face in bin bags and doorways; falling into patches of emptiness as the mirages faded. She missed him. Unsteady on her feet, Alice grabbed the essential supplies –

medicine, milk, yoghurt – for she did not have to play housewife this week – and fled back to her new home. Safely inside she shivered amidst all the undiscovered creaks and sounds, the neighbours' feet heavy on the stairs, the loud mannish shouts from the four Poles smoking in the garden, stretching their limbs outside of their cramped basement abode. Lulled by the hiss of the boiler and the fits and starts of the fan heater at her feet she thawed a little, additionally attempting to keep her chill at bay with the spare duvet, and ibuprofen caplets swallowed down with builder's tea.

Looking for the egg cup between coughing fits and nose blows, Alice instead uncovered old memories. She lingered over letters and photographs, lined up old snaps of herself, one in a Cornish harbour, one at night somewhere with the street lights glittering behind her, another with her hair hanging long down her back. She pulled her hand through her newly cropped do, nostalgic. Glimpses of her past inevitably led to others from Tim's. She was wary of looking too closely, after accidentally uncovering photos of his ex-girlfriend a few days previously. A woman who couldn't have been more different to Alice with her dark skin, tight curls and flat chest. A woman whose two-dimensional presence had sparked a row the night before Tim's trip. Alice shook her head at the memory, the sharp words, and hugged herself. She had been there before. For the first time in months she wished she had not quit smoking.

The egg cup was not among her pots of pens, pencils and paintbrushes, or under the messy piles of sketches and illustrations by her desk. It was not in the laundry basket, and the laundry was now loudly spinning itself clean in the washing machine, while she remained on guard in case of floods, as stipulated in the rental contract. A lot was stipulated in the contract. Alice was surprised it did not tell her what colour underwear she should put on, or at what times and in what positions she were permitted to have sex or, among its many bullet-pointed pages, where the egg cup had gone. The hunt had escalated to the improbable now. The missing item was not in Tim's sturdy suitcase with their hibernating summer clothes. It was not among the recycling, hiding behind the washed wine bottles, or under the ripped envelopes and pizza boxes. It was not in the under-used microwave, nor the dirty oven. It was not lolling in Alice's lingerie or boxing with Tim's shorts. Sweat patches grew clammy – dank and nastily odorous in between her breasts, and under each hot, sickly armpit. She had to lie down.

She closed the curtains in the bedroom, shutting out a city disappearing into the twinkling cloak of night below her. The unmade bed was stained with sex yet Alice could no longer smell Tim in the room and not only because of the symptoms of her illness. He had been there. The patterns of his left-behind shirts clashed mutely in his side of the canvas wardrobe, and beyond, her mismatch of sequins and brights were slip-sliding from their perches. His pile of dipped-into factual books balanced precariously on the bedside table, underneath her box of tissues, open paperbacks, lidless Biros, glasses of water, Strepsils and half-drunk Lemsips, but no egg cup and no Tim. He *had* been there, Alice told herself. Lying on his side of the bed she closed her eyes.

Alice didn't like to call Tim when he was away, her timing was always unfortunate – he would be going into a meeting, or out at the pub with colleagues. He would ring her later, he'd say, but he never did. By the end of the second day the loneliness hit her, and the worry. She would waver over the keys of her mobile, sometimes she would cry. Alice never called her friends at those times. She didn't want them to hear what she knew they would in her voice. She didn't want them to know that her new life in a new city with a new man was far from the perfect picture she had painted for them. They hadn't even met Tim. She doubted he would like them.

On the third day she opened the curtains in the office to find the pink flowers wilting, sagging towards the window ledge by Tim's desk; neglected. Beyond the glass, snow still clung to the path of the house opposite; weeping onto the pavement in the early morning sun. Alice pulled off the dead leaves, placed water in the tray, and moved it away from the ice cold window pane, the fierce winter bright. She muttered encouragement at the drooping leaves, the dropped petals. Hanging their entangled clothes to dry in the bedroom – shirt buttons hooked on lace knickers – she stared through the sash window to the city, frosty and clear below her, a sparkling blanket of rooftops snugly cushioned by strong hills. She gave in, scrolled to his name on the recent call list of her mobile. No answer.

Alice thought back to the night before Tim left – she could remember the silence, and then the awkward candlelit meal, but the remnants of their post-row reconciliation had become patchy. Tim had left for his trip quiet (and hungover) and what had become of the evening, the early hours, had returned to Alice in isolated snatches as she had gone about her day – some good, some not. In between the remembering there was the deliberate forgetting. The trying not to think about where Tim really was, not so much the Parisian business conference, but the people he was visiting while he was over there. His son. His ex. Killing two birds with one flight.

Caught in the intense glare of the bathroom, Alice splashed water onto her face and leant her weight upon her hands, resting on the basin. A tired woman stared back at her, puff-eyed and red-nosed. Bed-haired and crack-lipped. At her feet the bin was about to overflow with make-up wipes and toilet rolls, tampon wrappers and used sanitary towels. She left it as it was. It was easier to do that than to tell Tim each month that no, she was not pregnant and that yes she was sure. To see the second his face dropped before he caught it and pulled her to him. Before he kissed her forehead and held her tighter as their sighs escaped in unison. Her belly ached, long and low, like heartache, like loss. Every month brought a new period of bereavement, a red morning to mourn. She sank to the tiled floor and sobbed at her inadequacy as a woman, her barren salt-land of womb.

The cool white room calmed her fever and her thoughts. She sat there in silence for close to an hour. Just breathing and thinking. Breathing and thinking. It had been out of kindness that Tim had not put the photos of his son up in the flat, Alice knew that now. Kindness to their current situation and kindness because the baby snaps often included his son's mother, beaming, beautiful, complete. She should not have shouted. She wished she could take back the words she had yelled. She wished she were better able to control her temper when she was overwhelmingly upset, to diminish the inevitable regret. She figured, if she were going to sit there and wish for anything, it would be for her and Tim's wish to come true, a baby of their own, and a chance for him to do it right this time, a child they could love as much as they did each other.

She hadn't gone through the horror of tests yet. The doctor had been clear. Some women just take time to conceive after coming off their contraception. It was nothing to worry about. In fact she really should try not to worry, that wouldn't be doing her womb any favours. There was more advice: *Don't blame yourself, don't blame each other. Do talk. Don't smoke. Keep having sex. Take a holiday. Don't try so hard.* It didn't make it any easier. All around Alice friends were filling up like balloons for a kid's party. Engagement rings were flashing. Christening invitations burst out of envelopes and beckoned her to toyshops for gifts. Successful career or not, she was beginning to feel more and more like a failure.

Alice had wanted to hold off, to not rush things just as much as Tim. She had had her share of hang-ups and commitment panics along the way. Yet now her inability to conceive appeared to be a punishment for waiting. For holding off something Tim had already proved his prowess in. He'd got an A* twelve long years ago. Now she had to sit at excessive Welsh Sunday Lunches with his nieces and nephews, and that look his mother gave her, disappointed and expectant all at once. She couldn't meet it any longer. She made more and more excuses not to attend. Tim's son was a sworn secret, and one she would never ever break his trust upon, but the mother-in-law pressure had become too much for her to sit through for hours at a time. It left her feeling broken, useless.

A resolved Alice was on her hands and knees under the dining table, looking to see which nooks and crannies might contain her crockery, the still missing egg cup. As she peered into shadows Tim's parting words repeated on her. His rolling eyes. The deep sigh: 'Everything will be okay.' She had smiled weakly, meekly back at him and nodded. Reached up sleepily for a goodbye kiss, yet she had thought to herself that okay was not good enough, not even close. Alice changed her mind;

after Tim had left the need for him to be right – for things to be okay – had engulfed her more each day. New illustration commissions had been ignored and old ones delayed. She had to find it.

From under the dark awning of the dining table her eyes began to adjust to the light, and Alice looked beyond the blinking green eyes of the wireless router, the sprawl of wires leading past the dust gathered under the towers of Tim's CD collection, the neglected board games and wrapping paper to the broken storage heater. She gasped. For no good reason that she could think of, there it was. The egg cup, lolling on its side like a drunk surrounded by a shimmering halo of spilt salt crystals. She closed her eyes tight shut, counted to ten and then looked again. It really was there. Relieved, Alice reached for the egg cup with her left hand and, as she grasped it, her favourite familiar sound registered; that of the key scratching at and missing the lock. Attempting it again and then turning in the flat door. She jumped up, happy, and knocked her right temple on the underside of the dining table. When Tim walked in she grinned inanely at him, his face framed by dizzying stars.

Paying for Sex

1. She

Last night I paid for sex. When I met her she was wearing her
favourite red dress, the short clinging one with the spaghetti
straps. The one that hugs her hips; shows off those tanned,
toned legs. I'd made less effort, fraying at the edges in my
usual black cords, the same faded retro tee. We formed an
unlikely couple – a fashion league apart – but in that drop-
dead dress she fitted the bill and I paid it.

It was a sweltering summer night, a Friday. The club was packed
with perspiring party people and she was my third interest of
the evening; there must have been something in the recycled air.
The first, an undergraduate, all churlish curls and malachite
eyes, was taller than me but not bothered by it. Posing
confidently; the neon top was pulled tight, cropped at the midriff
to reveal a taut, pierced belly. I'd been debating leaving when
Green Eyes arrived; was ordering my 'one for the road' at the
bar. Had started too early, the talent was slow in arriving, and I
was bored amid a rainbow invasion of Ben-Sherman-shirty studs.
Out of nowhere, those smooth sapling arms were wrapping

themselves around my waist. They pulled me closer, suggestively. The licked lips full of promise as they breathed 'I've been thinking about you...' my way. I should have known better than to believe. Granted just one wickedly seductive embrace before I was discarded, dropped for someone sharper, funnier, richer.

The second was an old and regular companion who had one of those faces that could, in equal turn, be stunning, among the best-looking on Earth and then, without warning, monstrous – enough to kill the moment and the lover at the most inopportune of times. Last night, as we drew away from that first passionate encounter I saw ugliness and expectancy creep over that changeable face, the hungered chops. I didn't feel I could perform to such certainty. I realised that I didn't even want to. I let Monstrous Chops leave the club early and without me; turning my back on the sterling gaze, the confused, hurt expression to order and neck another drink.

Later, I strolled down the stairs and there she was, standing on the landing, in that red dress. She was perusing the throng of dancers, gossiping with her mini-skirted mates. Dressed up, girlishly over-the-top; hookers with high hems and low necklines. It was someone's boozy birthday celebrations. Their attire didn't surprise me – it was common to see them out dressed as grannies, trannies or first-time fannies, and I couldn't help but run my hand across the small of her back as I passed. She turned her head and fixed me in her gaze. A grin of recognition. A line of banter. A beat. I felt a heat rise from nowhere and dipped out of her brazen headlights, heading for the bar, throat dry.

2. (S)he

Ten years – that's how long we've been in each other's lives, (s)he and I. We met at university and yet sometimes, like last night and this morning, I can't find her name. It isn't teasing the tip of my tongue but caught, further back, like a dog hair or a dormant smoker's cough. One of my second year flatmates went to school with another of hers. We were studying at the uni while they were slacking at the art college. We all hung out, seven boys and seven girls, but not like that, not all of us. Only Lizzie and Jamie met publicly, regularly. The others paired off occasionally; secretly, casually. We never got it together, although it often crossed my mind. Sometimes (s)he'd stop me and smile, pausing a little too long over goodbyes at the end of the Student Union's weekly funk night; I think (s)he must have entertained the idea of me, of us, then too.

There was that party in our final year. I'd decided that that was the night, *our* night. The theme was Dead Famous; the venue, her house on Rhyddings Terrace. Every single one of the dead celebrities I'd arrived with was hammered – all three Michael Jacksons, Keith Floyd and Patrick Swayze – they'd started on the tequila early, but not me, couldn't touch the stuff after overdoing it at seventeen, before I'd even met Red Dress. I had soon discovered that a pyramid of 75p shots plus a fledgling-liver-in-training equalled projectile vomiting. I only had to catch a whiff to bring it all back again. Literally.

We'd both made an effort for that party – Red Dress and I – best costumes of the night I'd say; but then I would, I didn't see much of it. One minute we were flirting; it was definitely ON, the next I was outside spewing my guts up over her neighbour's petunias. It seems that someone had spiked the punch for a laugh – ha, ha. The first taxi wouldn't take me, and nor would the twelfth. A friend risked license and jail to roll their car down the hill from that Brynmill party to my Sandfields digs where I promptly passed out for the count in my puke-Pollocked clothes. I don't know what (s)he did, or where.

We never had another chance after that failed night. We

got ourselves other partners, finished university, moved on, only to both return to the familiar comfort of Swansea a few years later. We'd talk at parties and bars, have a laugh, act like the loaded expectancy of that long ago night had never happened. Act like mates. Last night was different. (S)he unnerved me with her sudden, blatant interest. It took me right back to that party night, that 'this is it' moment. It turned me cowardly. I decided to leave, to go and end the night with the dreg-ends at my small and seedy late night local. To sneak away unnoticed and stumble to slumber alone.

It's never that easy – I was halfway to the door when (s)he stopped me in my tracks. (S)he put on a comedy voice, wagging an index finger at me, hand on hip. 'Just wheeeeeeere do you think yooooooooou're going?' (s)he drawled and then pouted coquettishly. Foiled. The words, both admissive and inviting, left my mouth without permission and then, suddenly, Red Dress was linking arms with me, leaving too; folding those long athletic limbs into the waiting black cab. Her mates were left behind, tut-tutting in dismay, flicking cigarette ash with their traffic-light-red painted pointers. A warning sign.

At our destination I knocked on the glass three times, staccato, and the door open-sesameed. Inside the air was sour, saturated with disillusionment, populated with the dismal backwash of life. I was greeted with a grunt of recognition before a pint slammed down in front of me, half its contents flying into my face. I ordered a short for her, ice and sadly shrivelled slice. The locals were on their usual, sexually deprived, depraved form. 'Phwooaaaaar! Nice dress love!' they slurred, leering, winking at me, chortling with amusement at their own wit, my audacity. Someone pinched her arse. Another's fumbling fingers reached for and missed her chest. Downing my drink I realised I'd hardly been thinking straight. I took charge. Ushered her to the exit.

Outside (s)he began dialling a taxi – 'My place or yours?' – I should have seen that coming. I lived mere minutes away, and said as much. (S)he hung up and tottered behind me, complaining about her size 11 stiletto heels – 'the pain, the pain' – all the way.

3. He

Upstairs, in my Uplands flat, that heady flirtation reclaimed us and our clothes. We were naked in seconds. Skin on skin our genders reclaimed themselves, his man to my woman. Limbs entwined, entangled, stuck. For me, as quickly as the lust had arrived it faded. I was sobering up. His impassioned panic, the intensity of it, was leaving me uninterested, passive. I could see the face of my ex watching from the far wall and I felt guiltier than he ever will. Still, we fucked. Rushed and riskily. He insisted on looking at me face-to-face, on us holding each other's gaze till we came. He looked all wrong, I wanted to turn away, imagine someone else. At climax he shook, overcome, and I faked.

This morning his phone alarm rudely woke me from dreamland. He was all remorse, kissing me, blabbering on. Saying things like: 'You do know my situation, don't you?' They seemed like rhetorical questions. All his talk hurt my hungover head. I pretended to still be asleep, eyes tightly shut, my back to him. After a while he hushed, touched me, and pleased me enough to sleepily go at it again – anything to shut him up. Imagine the surprise when I came, we came, together. Then the incessant talking started up once more, his words tripping over themselves. He stopped and looked at me harshly, critically. I propped myself up on one elbow and squinted back, the day was too bright, had arrived too early. We were both undressed but he still felt the need to dress me down: 'You knew my situation and you just didn't care?' I couldn't be bothered to answer his incessant whine. There was nothing left worth saying back. Of course I knew. All our friends went to the wedding, all but me. Like last night I guess it slipped my mind. He doesn't wear underwear, and he wasn't wearing his ring.

His phone's ringtone screeched at us, a reminder that it was almost time for him to play 'parent with small children' again. Time to get home and shower before their train got in, before his chauffeur services were required. Daddy stropped about, angrily pulling on the red dress, preparing for the walk of shame. He thought better of it, picked up his mobile, dialled, spoke: 'Hello, yes, can I have a taxi from Uplands to Mount Pleasant... no, just the one... straight away please, yes...' And then to me, 'Where am I?' I told him the address. Walked him downstairs. Unlocked the heavy front door, flooding the dusty hall with sun. The street was eerily quiet as he kissed me quickly on the cheek, muttered a hurried, apologetic line: 'If I was happy with her it wouldn't have happened.' Then he descended the steps to the cab, barefoot, his stiletto heels in one hand. Opening the door he turned to wave, his face awkward beneath sharp stubble, his thick chest hair matted into clumps with the sweat of our sex. Awkward to be out of me, in drag and in daylight, his back turned on me and the cab door slammed. I could taste the metal divide.

Back inside I stripped my bed, my room, myself of the memory of him. I disengaged any emotional responses that were niggling beneath the surface, the misguided romantic aftermath of my orgasm. I knew how things were, how these things played out – I may have begun my days in the rubble of a wrecked home but I had not set out to be a home-wrecker.

I had no need for an affair – for sneaking around – and I had no need to become a single mother in punishment for a lousy fuck (and one good one). Scrubbed clean, I leave the house for the cashpoint and the shops. I pay my £25, dutifully, over the counter at the chemists. Answer routine questions in hushed tones with a flushed face to a weary yet pragmatic pharmacist; swallow the bitter pill. It turns out that last night will haunt me for the next three weeks, checking my knickers daily for their own, chemical, red dress. My mourning after our night before, a decade in the making.

Pica

The sandwich thief had struck again. The crook had taken no prisoners; just lunch. Five lunches in fact. A pesto pasta salad, some coronation chicken, a Weight Watchers pot of hummus and carrot sticks, one carton of Tuscan bean soup and a free-range egg mayo baguette. Tanja would have liked to ignore the whole farce, as she usually did with the moans about packed-up air conditioning, or meeting room double-booking, or any of the other day-to-day office hiccups. It was hardly plasma screens or laptops or stationery. The big boss wouldn't care about it. Not if the light-fingered one's loot bag was bulging with stolen staff lunches alone. Tanja would have liked to ignore it, but it seemed that food was important to her colleagues. Very important. Far more important than turning up on time or actually doing any work. And almost as important as the chance to watch Australian soaps on their lunch breaks. She gulped at the size of her e-mail inbox, watching its form spread out across her screen.

Moving her attention from her computer monitor, Tanja leaned back in her ergonomically designed chair and scanned slowly to the left and then to the right, eyeing the malcontent in her surround. Beyond her polished Perspex perch in reception the tension was palpable, hungered and brooding. Her mouth went dry. She got up for some iced water. The staff kitchen had begun to remind the receptionist of visits to her best mate's student house, where angered Post-it notes were stuck to cupboards about stolen cans of tuna and missing beer. The shelves in the fridge contained name-tagged pots of Marmite, Happy Shopper margarine and pints of milk.

Tanja had been working with the company for three years. She knew that proceedings had once been more civilised. Up until recently the staff fridge had been easy to manage and minimally stocked – milk (skimmed, semi-skimmed and soya), drinks for Friday's Wine Club and the occasional home-made lunch. That had all changed. First with company expansion, and then with staff gripes once the credit crunch had begun to bite. Colleagues had begun to snub the sandwich lady and copy Tanja's thrifty packed lunch ways. The fridge became overloaded with cheese and pickle rolls in identical supermarket bags. When Tanja went to clean it out each month she found new life forms growing. Some of the riled ranks were calling for mini fridges by each of their desks; mentioning unions and tribunals – all stuff and nonsense, of course, which would lead to nothing more than excessive, unnecessary paperwork. The gossips had started their Chinese whispers. They wanted to lynch the culprit and were pointing fingers at the emaciated temp in finance, or Pete who'd been thrown out by his missus just last week and couldn't cook up a decent cup of tea, let alone a meal. They cursed and cackled – the water cooler coven.

Tanja hadn't worried about the safety of her own lunch initially. The food that the thief had been concerned with had been either wrapped in Tesco bags or was the kind of generic supermarket sandwich or pasta salad that could have belonged to anyone. It could all easily have passed as an innocent mix-up – if it had only been one or two meals that had gone AWOL. Tanja used a kid's cartoon lunchbox to contain her own home-made grub. It was neon bright, and unmistakable. Plus she was pregnant. Six weeks into her second trimester, but the bad jokes had begun in earnest now that her skinny jeans no longer fitted her.

'Has your lunch gone missing yet love? No, well, I don't suppose they want gherkins and ice cream, *do they*?'

Tanja smiled back weakly. Gherkins were not on her list of cravings, in fact the very idea of them made her want to be sick, but, gazing longingly at the meeting room windows, she couldn't even begin to explain this. Smells had been sending her nauseous for weeks now – the usual things, like coffee, which was hazardous at the office, but also other bizarre triggers. Her evening primrose body cream brought memories of her mother up with the vomit. She would see her, all enforced-menopausal, in her nightie and hospital bed, a two-hour journey away from their family home. A hysterectomy before she was forty. A long silent drive, twice a week, with her 'non-smoker' stepdad – the painter. He drove one-handed, his other, nicotine-stained, trailed out of the open window. His car reeked of Special Brew, Polo mints, farts and Super Kings; it was littered with *Daily Mail*s and fogged by his Impressionist artistic illusions. She could see why her stepdad liked that art movement – he was also considered unfinished and insulting. A man of no substance, he hid underneath a paint-splodged ego using improvised bravado and bristling facial hair to hide his bad looks.

He had refused to wear a dressing gown when guests were staying. He appeared to like it when her school friends caught him walking to the bathroom naked in the middle of the night, although he didn't have the diamonds for exhibition, not even for doll's costume jewellery. She could see him years from now, dressed in nothing but a mac, maybe some well-worn boots, can in hand – lacking car, home and job – flashing at female students and nurses in the park. Then – later – dying in a gutter. It was more or less inevitable, if there was any justice to be had. Her usually chatty, nervous mother had seemed even paler, even more shrunken, there in that bed. Clucking about the poor, twenty-two-year-old lass in the adjacent cubicle and trying to distract everyone from her own pained face, especially herself. A hysterectomy to prevent the cancer that got her anyway. That caught up with her in the end. Tanja wished that she was still around.

Tanja didn't smoke, she'd tried it once and quite liked it but she was too afraid of The Big C. It was in the genes after all. She'd already had one scare earlier that year, a lump on her neck. At the start it resembled a raised gland, swollen like the ones she used to get at school when stressed out about a test, or an exam or some such. The GP, who was filming his examination of her, just ummed and ahed and prodded the protrusion. He looked quite disappointed, as he adjusted his glasses on his stubby nose and said he didn't know what it was. That more than likely it would go away. That she should come back in a month if it was still there. It didn't, and so she did. Afterwards the hospital called her in for an ultrasound twice. She went alone, waiting as people far older and sicker were wheeled in on trollies. When her turn came she sat on the bed for half an hour while various people wandered in and out to apply ultrasound gel, thick and clear like wallpaper paste, poke at her neck and examine the screen. They had all looked so serious. She had been surprised when they gave her the all clear. They'd had to repeat it to her three times before she got up to leave. Afterwards she went out and celebrated, and the result had been this pregnancy, and the tiny little ball of a creature that was growing inside her. Life breeding life.

She was content to be pregnant. There had been no doubt what she would do when the Clear Blue digital test had confirmed it. Tanja's mum and stepdad were divorced by the time she had passed away. Tanja got the house, and the car. She had a steady job, she would get maternity pay. She lived with her boyfriend, who was twenty-one and a plumber, and his family were supportive. Her best mate had told her she was throwing her life away, that she should have an abortion and dump Dean. That she should travel and learn – experience – but they were happy enough, Tanja and Dean. They liked their small, contained life. Their DVDs and pizzas and early nights. Painting the nursery and shopping for cots.

Her pregnancy had interrupted office life only as expected, some late entrances and rushed exits due to morning sickness and the need to purchase a few new work clothes; tops and dresses with a bit more give but no less style. Everything seemed to be happening just as the skim reads of her piles of pregnancy magazines informed her they would. Until now. Now she was flailing. She was becoming afraid to leave the house, or, when she made it to work, her desk. She didn't know what she might do. Nobody had prepared her for this. For licking windows with her tongue or chewing on soap, or worse, having the desire to guzzle down the stubby butts in her best mate's ashtray (for which willpower had prevailed thus far). No one had warned Tanja of the overwhelming desire, the overpowering need that would compel her to stop the car to consume handfuls of dirt grabbed greedily from the side of the road. Initially it had only been mild earthy substances she'd fancied, like the grubby potato peelings when making chips; things not so far removed from her daily diet, but then the need had grown stronger – crumbled bricks, twigs, those whole handfuls of soil. Driving to work her mouth would water just looking at the curving landscape, a savoury Willy Wonka paradise. Not one person had explained to Tanja how to negotiate the landscape without indulging herself during pregnancy. Her head would fill with desire and filthy thoughts as busty mountain ranges loomed towards her, more enticing than the dessert trolley at Crumbs. They would cause her to salivate and swerve in the road such that other drivers would beep and brake. To avoid causing a pile-up Tanja knew she would have to start taking the bus but then, as quickly as their onset, her cravings altered like a shift in season; her want latching onto products within her domestic landscape, moving indoors with her nesting instinct, straight into cuckoo territory.

Tanja didn't know who to talk to about it. She couldn't tell Dean. He'd think she'd lost the plot. Plus she'd never hear the end of it. Ever. He was a right wind-up merchant. She liked that about him. But not when it was aimed at her. What about family? Well family had died with her mother, as far as Tanja knew, and Dean's mum was obsessed with cleaning. If she cottoned on to what Tanja was eating she'd stop visiting them. She'd freak out. She would probably try to fumigate the place with Tanja in it. As for the expectant mum's best mate Julie, well she wasn't living up to her name so much now that Tanja couldn't come out on the lash. Julie was hell-bent on having a good time, with as many people as possible, and now that Tanja was not only not on the pull, but also teetotal, and a bit on the chubby side now you come to mention it, well to say she was being evasive would be... polite.

Instead of talking, Tanja became secretive. At home they would take it in turns to cook 'yellow food' (chips, waffles, cheese toasties, pizza) or call out for takeaway. Later she'd sneak her midnight snacks of soil from the garden or baking soda butties while Dean was sleeping. At work, in an attempt to disguise her increasingly odd and anxious behaviour, Tanja had taken to making her own packed lunch. Her colleagues, who were yet to copy her, simply thought she was being thrifty in the economic downturn. Little did they know that in between the innocent looking sheets of white bread and lettuce lurked the kinkiest special ingredients – at first it was coal, soil from the flower bed, or rusty nails and then later came seasonings of washing detergent or a salad dressing made from fabric conditioner. She felt like a secret smoker or filing cabinet alcoholic, spraying breath freshener down her throat in the loos and checking for give-away leftovers stuck between her teeth. There were only so many times she could smile meekly and mutter 'morning sickness' at nosy colleagues staring at her by the sinks. It would not do.

Despite feeling shiftier by the day, Tanja didn't really expect people to cotton on to her dirty little secret. Pregnant women have a bit of a reputation for acting bonkers now and again – hormones, see – so she didn't envisage any humiliating consequences on that count. It wasn't the first time Tanja had had such cravings, though it was her first pregnancy. She wondered if her little boy (or girl) would be like her. Making and eating mud pies and licking drain pipes at playtime. Tanja hadn't had the compulsion since she was a very little girl – she'd thought that she had grown out of it. She could barely remember doing it as a child, the memories came from stories her mum had told her accompanied by a younger laugh; broad and Brummie and full of heart. Her mother's hand pointing at faded curling photographs, evidence. Now, although she was aware that what she was doing, what she was putting in her mouth and consuming, was not the same as other people's diets, that it would be considered odd, and was probably not great for her future child, she couldn't seem to stop herself. It was compulsive and embarrassing and to make matters worse, the sandwich thief had now begun to take her lunch too. This worried her on two counts. One, was her filthy palate going to be uncovered? Two, how was she going to control her urges until home-time without her box of treats?

Tanja began to run through some options, things that could keep her going until she could leave the office. She sucked on the top button of her cardigan as she thought. She could go home sick, but she'd missed so many hours already and she wanted to avoid annoying her boss any more. She thought harder. It was already getting difficult to concentrate, and not only due to all the hormones racing around her body. She was an addict in need of her fix, but she didn't want to shoot up in front of all and sundry. She took a deep breath. There was the liquid handsoap in the toilets. That might work, as a quick hit. Or the cleaning products tucked in the bottom of the stationery cupboards. Or coffee granules straight from the jar. So transfixed by these thoughts was Tanja that she took a while to notice the stick-thin temp crying in front of her desk, and when she did she couldn't help but scowl at her.

'What. What is it?'

The girl didn't talk back, she wailed. Then finally she managed to spit out some words. Words like: *Ambulance. Call. Now.* And then she'd just keeled over. Turned white as the photocopier paper. They'd thought she was dead. But there was still a pulse. It turned out that Debbie in accounts had been coughing and spluttering since lunchtime.

Tanja dialled 999, as she had been trained to do in such circumstances, asked for the ambulance service, and then answered all their ensuing questions as best she could. She made sure that one of the designated first-aiders was with Debbie, and then took advantage of the commotion to nibble at some soap in the ladies. Temporarily sated and back at her desk she could hear the office a-buzz. The ambulance had already rushed Debbie to A&E. People were talking. Work had, as usual, been forgotten and little clusters of chit-chatters had pushed back their chairs, or perched themselves on edges of desks. It was like the week before Christmas or Friday afternoon might be. Tanja grabbed a file and walked slowly through the open-plan pods to the HR room. She caught snippets of the conversations as she passed.

'It had to be her.'

'But she is such a little thing.'

'I wonder what it was, that she ate that made her ill?'

'She might have had an allergy.'

'Damn stupid helping herself to other people's lunch if she did.'

'Maybe that's why she did it. A food roulette. Maybe she had a death wish.'

'She has been right moody lately.'

Tanja felt herself starting to retch. She turned quickly on her heel, as she had become so practised during her morning sickness, and marched back to the ladies, throwing up bile and blue soapy fluid into the sink. Amazingly, nobody else saw. She rinsed out her mouth and wiped down the ceramic basin as what she had just heard was digested by her mind. Of course. Tanja thought of what she had concocted for herself in the early hours, the grey of dawn, while Dean snored through dreamland upstairs. Had Debbie been poisoned by the detergent and blueberry mousse? Or the couscous salad glinting with crumbs of coal and shards of stone, the mica of the granite gravel. For the unpractised that wouldn't just break a filling. It could hurt on the way down. It might tear or perforate your insides, or block them up, if you weren't careful. Like a drain. You don't even want to know what they would do at the other end, if they made it that far. It wouldn't be pretty, that's for sure. Why did these concerns not crop up when Tanja ate these things for herself?

She wondered if Debbie knew which lunch had caused the

damage. If her colleague was going to survive. If Debs didn't, would the police come along pointing their fingers at her, Tanja? Should she say that she had done it on purpose, to catch the culprit, or would that lead to her being prosecuted for poisoning? As her head started to spin with all the questions and more nausea, the door to the toilets sprang open.

'There you are, Tanja,' shrilled the big boss's deputy, Carmen. 'You're not doing that...' she paused, and pulled a face, 'pregnant throwing up thing again are you?' She sniffed the air.

'No, no. I'm fine!' Tanja said back, too cheerfully.

'Good, well I need you to help me out with a couple of things. I have an enormous mail-out that should have been sent yesterday, and then there's the Debbie dilemma...'

Tanja raised her eyebrow. 'Oh?'

'Well Liz from Accounts just called from the hospital. Anyway it turns out that the little incident of the sandwich thief has been solved.'

'Was it...?'

'Yes, yes, keep up. Only, well there's a small matter that would be better if it didn't get out.'

'Well they think that she must have swallowed some poisons, cleaning fluids and the like, a cry for help. Of course she's denying it, but there's no other possible explanation...'

Still feeling weak, Tanja had begun to zone out again. She hadn't eaten enough for one, and certainly not for two. She was looking at the full-length mirror opposite, nailed into the white tiled wall, entranced by how the light danced off it. She thought it would feel cool against the skin. She reached out and touched it lightly with her fingers. But that wasn't enough. She stepped forward and stuck out her tongue. Licked the glass. It tasted good. Like diamonds. It sparkled, fizzed and tingled in her mouth. She did it again, repeatedly lapping at her wet reflection, and that of Carmen's face, aghast.

Sauce

Some things go better together; coupled up, two by two, like animals for the ark. In Joe's mind these included his parents, Mulder and Scully, ketchup and chips, a cuppa and the crossword, a pint and a fag – he stopped. He had wanted to say Flora and Joe, but he knew that wasn't true, for her at least. Now Flora and her bright yellow trench coat, they worked; as did Vic and Bob, sweet and sour, The Handsome Family, Page and Plant, and Roobarb and Custard. Joe was an unfussy chef; he liked to see how two flavours worked with one another without overpowering the final dish; he understood the magic of simplicity within the kitchen. His regulars were as set in their ways at eighty as he was at thirty. Neither was that fussed on change.

The cogs of Flora's mind worked differently: as she saw it things went better in groups, multiples, double figures. Pairs induced yawns, the well-worn coupling just waiting to be separated, each half abandoned like forlorn odd socks. She liked things bigger, more fluid, less contained than the mundane union of two people, of him and of her. She wanted to hear the noise of a full band, eccentric and screwball, like Of Montreal, Micachu & The Shapes or Tilly And The Wall.

Rainbow bright and punch pop stomp-strop shiny, happy and true. Loud and unmissable. This was why she liked eating amidst the crowds at Joe's. She pushed open the door.

Joe removed his steamed-up glasses, wiped the lenses and placed them back on his nose. The café was busy, lunchtime primetime, chattering voices, clattering crockery, clinking cutlery, the whir and splutter of the temperamental coffee machine hissing over it all. Catching a glimpse of the unmistakable English mustard-coloured jacket in the corner of his scratchy eye meant that Flora was here. Joe needn't have seen it to notice her sunny voice chiming clear above the mingled mutters of others. She was in high spirits, swapping gluttonous gossip with the plump, home-permed Eileen, distracting her from her waitressing. He braved a slightly longer glance, took in her petite form, the sleek knot of cappuccino locks, those dark, gravy eyes, before he ducked back into the relative calm of the kitchen to cook up: 'Eggs, chips and beans, twice', 'Welsh rarebit,' a student house's 'All day breakfast' and the latest office couples' clichéd love ritual of a 'Chocolate sundae, two spoons'. By the time the rush had died down and he could nip out the back for a chipped mug of coffee and a fag there was no sign of Flora; he couldn't even detect the delicate jasmine scent of her above his ever-present odour of stale chip fat and nicotine.

Joe realised that Flora hadn't stayed to eat; he'd have noticed the quirks of her order – 'Jacket potato, cheese and beans (cheese first), pickle, smile'. or 'Vegetarian breakfast, extra egg, half beans, half tomato (tinned), to eat to Jeff Buckley's Grace album.' Plus he had always let her eat there half price – he still did even now she was doing well for herself – so Eileen would draw his attention to an order from Flora by marking the corner with a ballpoint daisy, or, teasing, a bright red heart. The truth of it was Joe could barely speak to Flora these days: the crush had become so crushing. He'd stutter a hello and act busy instead. That's why, the next time she comes in, he does little to draw her attention to himself, hot and greasy after another busy lunchtime shift.

It was quieter, 3 p.m. in the afternoon, so he was helping to clear tables, chatting to the regular pensioners having their cups of tea and cake, their half-a-tuna sandwich, when the bell announced her entrance. She smiled in Joe's direction, and then waltzed to the counter with a pile of her latest DIY fanzine regally held out before her. There she swept all the other leaflets to one disorganised corner and proudly arranged hers in a flamboyant curve. He overheard her telling Eileen how not one but two of her editors had actually paid her on time for her photographs. She was going to celebrate with...

'Mushroom omelette and chips, a big pot of home-made ketchup, a mug of strong coffee and one of Joe's cigarettes, please love.' Usually his cue to get cooking, but instead Joe took his time.

Flora chattered some more with Eileen and the girls at the counter, offering suggestions as they went to change the music. Engrossed, she appeared not to notice the balding shadow of a man as he slid in from the street to stand mere inches behind her; lips pursed, palms sweating. Joe watched as she coolly asked Eileen if she could be a love and bring her coffee over to Table 10, it would give her a chance to take the weight off after delivering her fanzine all over town on foot, to have another proud read of it herself. He saw how Flora hoisted her bags higher up her arm, and, with one quick glance over her left shoulder walked slowly, quietly towards the corridor, the ladies toilet.

'I'll wait for you here, Flora, shall I?' Sweaty growled menacingly. She didn't look back or reply. She was gone a while. The man paced while he waited, flustering the remaining customers enough for Joe to seat him at the table with Flora's cooling mug of coffee, tasting the quart of whisky upon his hot, angered breath and feeling the glare of his urine yellow, reptilian eyes.

Eventually Joe cut through the kitchen to the toilets to find that the ladies were deserted and the back door to the patio was ajar. He crept through it and whispered her name. Joe knew the man wasn't the kind to give up that easily; he'd look for her out here, and if she were hiding there'd be trouble. Joe didn't like trouble. There was no answer. The back gate was wide open onto the street behind, and as he went to close it Joe spotted a sunshine-bright streak of a girl, Flora, speeding down the network of alleyways opposite, soon out of sight. He locked the gate, picked up an empty crate from the stack, and walked back onto the premises just as the man, face flushed with rage, appeared.

'Flora?' he bellowed, barging past Joe and storming down the corridor, thumping the open door to the empty ladies toilet. Joe scurried back into the kitchen out of the way. Busying himself stirring sauces and loading the dishwasher he heard Sweaty slam his way around the staff toilet, the gents and then finally outside.

'Fuck's sake, Flora,' the man had yelled to no one in particular before heading back through the café to the busy shopping street to roar down his mobile. Call over, he huffily climbed back into his badly, madly parked car to slump at the wheel, head in hands, before starting up the engine and driving on, restoring Joe's place to a Flora-less peace, gentle chit-chat and a stereo murmur of Richmond Fontaine. Joe took a moment between orders and downed a tepid coffee. He smiled – that was Flora all over, that. She couldn't smell the difference between sage and rosemary but she could sniff out danger, and when she did, she ran. She ran fast. When the café phone rang he knew it was her. He lifted the receiver to hear Flora's lovely voice shaking down the line, the gasps between strings of words. Joe could tell she'd been crying, delicate flower, and he knew why. He often thought he knew her better than she knew herself.

'Joe, hon, I'm sorry, did you cook the omelette? I'll pay for it if you did. I will. I promise.' Her snotty words ran into one another. 'I had to run away. You worked that much out, right? I gave my yellow coat to a tramp on the way and I'm hiding out in a windowless pub by the prison, chain smoking with all the other escaped convicts pulling sad panda faces. Do you remember him?'

Of course he did. The rage machine was Flora's ex-landlord from the tiny basement flat she had run out on last summer. Someone else that didn't go well with Flora, as it happened. She swore she didn't owe any rent, well maybe £50, £100 at most – and the deposit she'd left, unclaimed, would cover it and then some. After two years of her living there on her own and paying the rent on time, no hassle, he had started yelling at her in the street for no reason. She would walk away la-la-la-ing, covering her ears with her hands like a kid, avoiding the scene. It didn't stop there. He started showing up at her door at all hours, drunk. Letting himself in when she was sleeping, while she lay passed out, half naked on her sofa or in her bed. He didn't actually do anything, as far as Joe had managed to ascertain, just stood there watching her, which was creepy enough. When Flora woke one night to find him there, staring, she screamed and he scarpered; she'd bagged up less than half of her possessions that very night and walked out. Walked all the way to Joe's doorstep. Turned up with sad dog eyes, with FRAGILE stamped across her forehead, and he had let her in, let her stay. She hadn't wanted to go to the police about her ex-landlord and Joe hadn't pushed her to. He thought the drama would soon settle down. He had hoped that he and Flora might too.

Each day Joe's heart had weighed heavier, as Flora made herself quite at home, encased within the four walls of his life. Oblivious, she gave him the odd, completely platonic hug but not a hint of love, or a scrap of hope. Instead she worried. She bit her nails. She ignored her mobile which had rung thirty, fifty times a day as her ex-landlord left increasingly threatening messages. She was more nervous than Joe had ever seen her. She shook and she hid. Even after Joe bought her a new phone Flora still wouldn't go out much; instead she lay on the sofa day and night, smoking all of Joe's tobacco with the electric glow of the TV flickering over her face, eyes open, eyes shut. She seemed drab and unrecognisable, full of fear.

Joe understood. Flora had always hated scenes. Show her a confrontation and she would do pretty much anything to avoid it, to stop her mates' from effing and blinding, kicking off, and if she couldn't stop them, or if the yelling and animosity were aimed at her, she'd disappear. Just like that. She wouldn't actually leave town, she wasn't brave enough, and so although she'd bolt out on you without a word, she'd rarely have gone far.

Flora's fresh starts only ever involved a new neighbourhood of the city and an altered identity in the form of a haircut or wardrobe staple. She rarely traded in her friends, though she might swap the stomping ground of her social life until whatever it was she had run from had blown over, move from the live scene to the dance scene, the clubs to the house parties, or from there to the highbrow set, art galleries and book groups, the theatre, science café lectures. She would shape-shift until the bad relationship, broken friendship, or regrettable drunken outburst she'd run from had been forgotten, or overshadowed by someone else's misfortune, heartbreak or stupidity. It was a small-town vibe of a city, but it wasn't a village. These things dissipated soon enough. After a month cocooned at Joe's place a more confident and calm Flora emerged, ready to face the world; moving on but not out of his life. She enrolled in a college course, immersing herself in web design and coding html, new spaces and new friends.

Nine months have passed since then, and Flora has only just begun to wear her yellow trenchcoat out again, attempting to return to her old image, her old life. Unfortunately for Flora her beady eyed ex-landlord appears to still hold a torch for her. Or just a grudge. She is still prattling down the phoneline to Joe about the earlier incident in the café. Ignoring Eileen's glares, he found he wasn't really listening to Flora's words either. He was happily lost in a daydream of two by two. He was thinking about how Flora didn't know what he knew. She didn't know how certain things were just better together, like his parents, like Mulder and Scully, like Flora and her yellow coat, Flora and him. On the other end of the line Flora was thinking about packing her bags. She was wondering why Joe hadn't protested when she had told him she was leaving town for good. As the three beeps indicate that her mobile battery has died, Flora decides that Joe must know what she knows. As the line between them cuts off, Flora thinks that Joe must agree with her. He must know that moving city is the right thing to do, and – like her and the mustard trenchcoat – that some things worked better apart.

A few drinks later Flora is back in her room. She is packing her bags. She gathers together her few prized possessions and piles them into her rucksack. She empties and turns off the fridge, the heating and all electrical appliances. She ties a ribbon around her *X-Files* box set and leaves. The keys drop on the mat behind her. Halfway to the station she stops at

Joe's flat, places the DVDs on his back doorstep by the recycling bins, a parting gift. She turns again, hoists her bags higher up her shoulder and walks on, out of the garden, sticking her thumb out as she reaches the road. She wants her first lift to be in a red car. She does not care where it takes her. She does not look back.

Big on Japan

Fred was big on Japan. He wished that his band would make it over there, but couldn't escape the ear wiggle niggle that they weren't going to make it anywhere. Mainly because they hadn't made it out of the drummer's garage. In nine years. Despite this minor obstacle to his dream life, Fred was swotting up on the archipelago. He consumed reams of contemporary Japanese fiction from Yoshimoto to Murakami and longed for eternal bus journeys alongside snow-capped mountains, and nights singing karaoke or stalking street vending machines for beer and used schoolgirl knickers.

He drank sake and Asahi, when staying in or going out. He knew the Wagamama menu off by heart, but mainly subsisted on instant noodles and Japanese junk food picked up from the oriental supermarket on the high street in luminous plastic just-add-water pots. He was addicted to wasabi highs and Pepsi Ice Cucumber, miso soup and supermarket sushi. He googled new trends in culture religiously and liked to daydream about a change of career – opening a Cat Café or becoming a geisha boy. He had killed forty-three Tamagotchi and climaxed many more times than that while watching manga porn, despite all the octopi.

His sister called him an idiot. It was her ritualistic way of starting the day. At home, when they were teenagers, she would waltz down to the table, grab the canned coffee from him and say 'Idiot' often followed by 'Prat', 'Wanker' and 'Gay Lord.' A jabbing finger. A smirk. Now that they had evolved into adult form, and lived in separate studio flats rather than their childhood box rooms she would call his mobile first thing instead. 'You are an idiot. Have a crap day.' He knew something was up if the call didn't come. She was the anti-hostess and he used her routine insults as his alarm for work. It was good to wake up that way, it prepared you for the day ahead, put you in your place, stopped you from getting any illusions that life could be good, that you might not be an idiot. Why set yourself up for such a fall? He considered renting her out. It would probably catch on in Japan.

When Fred's sister wasn't calling him an idiot, she would say other things. Often about his obsession with the Land of the Rising Sun. It enforced her idiot theory, and her thesis that suggested he was an eighties throwback. She said he was stuck in a time warp. That he should swap sushi for Afghan food as that was where it was at now, or the credit crunch chic indulgence of value ready-meals: microwave lasagne or shepherd's pie eaten ironically at dinner parties, served up in their individual containers and shovelled into hungry mouths with the snap together plastic cutlery, the forks and childproof knives that couldn't cut a thread let alone a corner. He embarrassed her. She said. When she started slagging off Japan he would drift off, would imagine having *asobi seksu** with the New York band's keyboardist Yuki Chikudate.

Fred didn't look Japanese. He looked like a Viking or a bassist in a heavy metal band from the late eighties. He could have cropped up on Kerrang! TV, or in *The Adventures of Asterix*, and you wouldn't have thought anything of it, but if he'd turned up in *The Ring*, the original version, well he would have scared you. Fred had a lot of ginger hair. In places you would expect it, like his scalp and above his eyes, and also in places you'd rather not find it, like on his shoulders and up his nose. He couldn't be more different from his Rat Pack namesake if he tried.

His father liked crooners, apparently. Fred couldn't know for sure. He was only a baby when his dad had lived with them for a few nights of every week, the rare weekend. Fred was not even walking when his dad had left for good. 'He's gone to Japan, love,' his mum would answer, when Fred asked why his daddy didn't come and see them any more. She'd point to it on the inflatable globe in his bedroom, trace her fingers east from their city across the oceans and land to the other side of the world. She thought this would be easier, but of course more questions would come: 'But why doesn't he write to us, Mum, or send postcards?' 'He's very busy, Freddie, he's a very busy man.' His sister would jab him in the ribs when their mother turned back to her book or the TV. 'Idiot!' she would hiss. 'Re-tard. He's left us.' Fred chose to believe his mum over his sister. His sister was always saying things that weren't true. She was always blaming other people, usually him, for the bad things that she had done.

On a whim, one Saturday, when Fred was trundling into town, he decided to get a tattoo. He hadn't ever had a burning desire to get one before that moment but the petite pink-haired girl on reception had caught his eye as he'd glanced through the window and she had smiled. He found himself walking in, through the double doors, right up to her. 'Can I help?' she had asked him. He had ended up walking out of there an hour later with a tattoo branded upon the flabby skin of his left upper arm, all red and scabby. It was the Japanese symbol for luck and he hoped it would bring him some. He hadn't felt very lucky when he was having it done. It was all he could do not to scream. Or faint. He didn't want the girl on reception to hear him being a wimp. Katie her name was. She also worked on the door of the rock club he sometimes went to with his band mates. She'd said she'd let him in for free that night, if he wanted. He did.

Between the girl, and the relief, the buzz he had from the tattoo, he had felt ecstatic walking the rest of the way into Bristol to his destination – Forbidden Planet. His mind had filled with the possibilities of the evening, distracting him from the comic-lined paradise of his favourite store. He'd called up Paul, the singer from the band, and they'd eaten Seafood Ramen and decided they really ought to book a gig soon, to get out there. That they were going to make it out of the garage and onto the cover of *Kerrang!* That Fred and the band would make it big in Japan. Fired up on all this fighting talk of success and new guitars they had gone to the pub and sunk a few pints of cider before parting ways, Paul to his girlfriend's and Fred to the rock club. To Katie.

At the club, good as her word, Katie let him in for free. He said he'd bring her a drink down later, as thanks. The gig was a good one, sweaty and noisy, the drums pounding through his torso as he jumped around, resonating through his rib cage, his lungs. When the DJ took over, Fred had gone to the bar and then back down to the girl with pink hair on the door. He had passed her a drink and they had argued amiably about music for a while. The human traffic was quiet so he took her another drink and then another.

Later, when he had leaned in closer, expecting a kiss, Katie had laughed and patted his arm. She'd looked up at his confused face and widened her small, dark eyes. 'Don't you know who I am Fred?' she had asked. It was clear that he did not. She had taken a swig from her pink alcopop and considered this. She'd finished her drink, exhaling the words as she'd pulled the empty bottle from her glossed lips: 'I'm your half-sister, Freddie.' She'd grinned but Fred's face had crumpled. He had started to tell her that she couldn't be but then his beer daze had cleared and he'd realised that she could. That he now knew what his mum had meant when she'd said that his dad had gone to Japan. She'd meant that he had gone back to his other family, just like his whole sister had always said he had. He'd left them for a house on the new estate with his pretty Asian. Katie seemed lovely, incestuously lovely, but Fred didn't feel so big on Japan any more. He didn't feel very lucky either.

Asobi Seksu is colloquial Japanese for 'playful sex'. It is also a dream-gaze indie band based in New York.

Waxing, Waning

Natalie forced her eyes open a slit. Through the salt-crust of sleep gripping her lashes she could see a slice of faded beach hut – beams of early morning bright casting spotlights upon the dancing dust – and there, beyond the end of her long sunburnt legs, just out of reach of her grazed left foot, her new bikini bottoms were shimmering like a mirror-scaled fish drying out in the Thai sun.

Although she was naked from the waist down Natalie didn't panic. Jen had seen her starkers – or near enough – plenty of times over the years, sharing toilet cubicles in pubs and clubs, or trying on the entire contents of her wardrobe before a night out. Waking up somewhere that was not their beach hut had also been getting to be a bit of a habit lately. They had chosen unwisely in booking their resort, in actually bothering to make a reservation at all, so it seemed, but there was no chance of a refund so they stuck with it. On the upside their part of the island had the best beach for swimming and sunbathing by far, but on the downside it was the furthest away from the travellers' bar they spent most of their time hanging out in, and even further again from the party segment, where Norwegian, Swedish and American students, tall and bronzed, larked about in the water, and flashed long, lazy smiles their way.

More often than not Jenny and Nat would wake up in one of the unused chalets attached to the traveller hang-out they so liked, or upon the floor mats of its bar, the kindly placed mosquito net whipped off them, and two cool beers placed into their hands with an insistent urge from lopsided toothy gums to get moving before the young families filled the booths up for breakfast. The two friends would head back to their hut to swim in the tropical shallows and then shower; to drink banana shakes in the shade; to doze and dip, doze and dip. Some days they would hire scooters and race around the island exploring, occasionally sliding off, grazing elbows, knees. Other days they would jump onto the open-backed taxis, hopping off again to find waterfalls in the jungle, riding weary elephants or clamouring across risky rocks to swim with local families in the natural pools. Then they would eat a picnic on the bank of a stream as they waited for enough people to fill up a taxi to take them further up the island or back to base.

Natalie hadn't slept in the bar this time though, but nor was she in one of the crash-pad chalets that were becoming so familiar to her escape from slumber. She allowed her half-conscious mind to drift. Her memory of the later events of the night was still too hard to reclaim; instead her thoughts turned to the new metallic bikini that now lay at her feet. Buying it was a celebration. A line in the sand. A new start. She remembered going into town shopping despite all the contrary advice online, comments on travel blogs and Gumtree and the like which had implored visitors to 'wait until you get there'. Natalie knew that she would be able to buy ten bikinis in Thailand for the price of one off-season at home but she didn't want to leave her wardrobe staple for the next three months to chance. This was the first holiday she had had since she was small. The first bikini she had dared to brave since primary school and her first time travelling, or doing anything very much, by herself. Free from family and a string of controlling boyfriends. Just her and Jenny. Friends forever. Blood sisters – safe together – sworn on each other's lives.

When Natalie had seen the bikini the month before, shiny and new, in the local surf shop she had known it was The One. She had been embarrassed to ask to try it on but Jenny had insisted. She felt shy standing naked, not more than a metre from the counter, with only a thin sarong curtain to hide her modesty. There were mirrors all the way around the cubicle. It was like the unforgiving 360-degree mirror – 'the fat room' – in her mum's favourite TV show, *Trinny & Susannah*. Except that, whatever Natalie's spiteful mother told her, and whatever her no-good boyfriends had reinforced, Natalie wasn't fat. In fact up until a couple of months ago Natalie had been the opposite, far too skinny and gaunt. She had worn the tabloid pallor of someone who survives on cocaine, dirty and violent sex, alcohol and verbal abuse. On two meals a week, forced down to appease a screaming gut, a scoured throat. On that shopping day Nat was unrecognisable from the person she had shrunk into over the previous two years; it was a healthier, curvier woman who pirouetted and grinned back at her reflection. How different her face looked at the correct angle from the mirror, not looming in to a close-up vertically above it with a note hanging from a red raw nostril. Her empty pupils were no longer the insatiable black holes, hungry for more, and more, and more. That need that she had carried for the drug and the man who supplied it to her lay dormant, but the fear that it would resurface at any time remained.

With all this in mind, initially Thailand had not appeared to be a wise choice as a place for them to get away from it all and avoid the drugs, but it fitted the rest of their criteria in that it was cheap and it was very far from home. You certainly couldn't pick out the industrial coastline of Port Talbot from there. Nat wanted to have a laugh and have a drink, but Class As, class-anything were off limits. No full moon parties and no life sentence in a Thai prison, thanks. So she thought and so Jen insisted. Neither of them planned on doing a Claire Danes in *Brokedown Palace*. They chose the serenity of Elephant Island (Koh Chang) instead. The island that never forgets was, by all accounts, a sleepier and less tourist-frequented place than the tacky trappings of Koh Samui; they decided that it would be far easier to sidetrack the Thai holiday hedonism there, and if all else failed then they would hop the border to the stricter realms of Cambodia, and go from there to Laos and Vietnam. They would keep going until their money or visas ran out.

With their get-away destination decided, and new passports issued, they set off. A long flight to Bangkok led them to one night of restless sleep in a noisy hostel above the 24-hour hustle and bustle on the Koh Sahn Road. A taxi took them to the airport where the sweetest internal flight and one short minibus ride got them onto the ferry. There, as the island came into focus ahead of them, lush and magical, the troubles they had left behind dropped from their shoulders, bouncing into the turquoise waters. Their whole faces burst with waxing crescent grins as they clinked their bottles of beer together and leaned on the railings; taking photos and pointing.

Natalie's head was pounding with more than the habitual SangSom hangover that she was learning to expect. Her mouth felt like a skunk had died in it and was rotting right there on her tongue. The temperature in the hut was turning up to simmer and there was no extractor fan, no air con. She needed something to drink. She needed to get back to her hut. She tried to move, but every limb felt heavy, pinned down. Her skin lay tender upon the splintered wooden boards. It was a familiar feeling – the pain and bruising, the forgetful fog of the night before, like so many others with ex-boyfriends; her ex-fiancé, especially. If it weren't for the heat she would have mistakenly believed he was there, beside her, everything as it used to be, before she broke off the engagement, before she got on a plane. All the good, the unravelling of knots that the holiday had so far allowed her began to snap and retract; her gut tightening, her heart rate quickening, struggling. She could hear someone else sleeping nearby, but her neck ached and she couldn't turn to see if it was Jenny. It didn't sound like her. The breathing was deeper, gruffer, and male. She spoke her name: 'Jenny? Jenny are you here?' The person to her right stirred but didn't wake. Natalie closed her eyes again and tried to remember.

It was New Year's Day. For the last night of the year Jenny and Nat had taken their routine early evening swim before showering and switching to dry bikinis, sarongs, flip-flops and vest tops. They had eaten – Pad Thai for Jen, Pineapple Rice served in a boat made from the fruit's carcass for Nat – on the beach under a full-bellied moon. Their lopsided table had lurched towards the sea, and then so had they, to buy paper lanterns and scribble their wishes for the new year, sending them flaming into the sky like fireflies, their future dreams ablaze. Hugging each other, laughing, the best friends had stumbled on to a bar with bright cushions and low tables, coloured lights snaking around it. There they had polished off buckets of SangSom and Red Bull, racing to the bottom with straws, wearing the cocktail umbrellas as accessories in their hair. 'Good riddance!' They had chanted. To Jen's ex-boyfriend, Nat's ex-fiancé. To all the broken sections of their lives that they hated. They told each other how it would all be different when they went back home, *if* they ever went back. Happy, they drank more, swaying along the sand from bar to bar, arm in arm.

'Jenny?' croaks Natalie once again. No answer. The breathing beside her doesn't alter at all. She manages to shift her weight, to glance to the other sleeping body. A Thai man is lying on his back about a foot away from her. She doesn't recognise him. He looks older than the boys from the bar, and several of his teeth are blackening in his slack jaw. His presence jars something in her mind, still out of reach. It makes her feel uneasy and she scans the hut for Jen, and for the remainder of her things. It has little furniture – simply the mats they are lying on and one stool. A couple of guitars prop up one corner and some small, childish paintings dot the walls. A movie-clip of a memory returns to her – Jen walking away, back to the hut, clutching her head. Under attack from a migraine. Her face is apologetic when she whips around to face Nat. 'Have fun,' she mouths and then turns again, walks on.

Nat looks down at her body. Her vest and bikini top are skewiff, one white triangle of breast pokes out between the two items of clothing, the nipple exposed. She rearranges herself and quietly pulls on the remainder of her clothes – the bikini bottoms, the sarong. Wincing, she stuffs her flip-flops into her shoulder bag and sneaks out the door. A couple of locals snigger as she passes, causing a paranoid Natalie to break into a run, twisting down and right to the shore where, gaining her bearings, she slows to a jog all the way across the three beaches and back to her resort. Inside their hut Jen is snoring noisily. Nat brushes the excess sand from her feet, crawls under the sheet on her side of the double mattress and closes her eyes.

The splutter of the fan alerts Natalie to the fact that Jen is getting up. She keeps her eyes shut – an undercover agent. She listens as Jen puts on suntan lotion, and as she leans over Nat's body and asks if she is awake. She feigns sleep as Jen kisses her cheek, whispers 'Happy New Year!' and puts a cold bottle of water on the floor beside her. She stays there, motionless, as Jen heads out for her morning swim. Natalie counts for one minute after the hut door closes behind her friend, and then she sits up too quickly and, head spinning, begins to work methodically through the routine she has been plotting since she returned to her hut. She can smell the unfamiliar man on her skin, lingering like cheap cologne, as she strips from last night's clothes. She showers, rinsing sand out of the cuts and scratches lacerating her epidermis, the soap stinging her bruised and sunburnt layers as she scrubs. She refuses to cry. Instead she examines the damage clinically, and tries to shift the big black blank that is preventing her from knowing what had actually happened to her. Whether that man had had sex with her, and whether she had wanted him to. Bruises bloomed violet upon the blushing flesh of her new-found curves. She tried to shut down that side of her mind, to partition the events of the previous evening, the blank hours, off from everything else; to lock it out of sight and out of mind. Out of existence. A black hole of bad decisions and bad times. 'Smile, it may never happen...' and yet it probably had.

Wanting to camouflage her injuries and to avoid questioning from Jen, Nat pulls on some recently purchased fisherman trousers and a light, long-sleeved top. She covers the small cut on her temple with a scarf, pops her contraceptive pill into her dry mouth, and downs the bottle of water Jen had left her. She pulls on her sunglasses and moves out to the porch to see her travel buddy just walking out of the water lower down the beach. She waves. An intent volleyball game is well under way to her right. Natalie settles herself into the hammock, rocking gently. She looks out to the point where sky meets sea, no other land in sight, and makes a pact with herself. The few hours between Jen and Natalie getting separated simply didn't happen. She would spin Jen a tale involving dancing, and a guy who she had liked leaving with another girl. She would grin and say, 'But what does it matter? That was last year.' Natalie would tell this tall story so well that she would convince herself that that was what really happened, and that today was just like waking up after innocently passing out at a party the night before, like she had so many times with Jenny in their teens. It was nothing. She would allow herself to remember the incident just once, back in Wales, at the GUM clinic, the fingers of both hands crossed, and then she would forget all about it. Let it slide to nothing, wane to a darkened moon. A secret for the elephants.

'Happy New Year!' she yells, throwing her arms around Jen as she appears on the porch dripping with saltwater. Her friend cocks her head to one side – 'No hangover? What time did you get back?' Nat grimaces and buries a shell under the drifted sand with her toe. Ignoring the second question, she replies: 'Oh, only a very teeny one.' She wrinkles her nose. 'Okay, okay, you win, it's massive, but despite this pounding impediment to my brain I have been thinking. We should bail on this hut for our last night, stay in one of those places in the jungle at the other end of the island for the night, hang out in that hippy bar you love that juts out over the ocean. You in?' She looks at Jen with jet black eyes, hungrily expectant for her nod of approval. Instead her best friend looks nonplussed. 'We could leave the bags here and pick them up on the way to the ferry tomorrow?' she pleads. Like her scribbled lines upon their paper lanterns the night before, Natalie had a childlike need to believe in wishes coming true. She wanted this to be the year of the new bikini. Her year. The year where things changed.

Flap, Flap

'I'm feeling fine, filled with emotions, stronger than wine, they give me the notion...'

That's Doctor Slack. He's always singing. Always happy, he says. Nobody is *always* happy. Nobody is *ever* happy here, we're just *alright*. Medicated and alright. Thanks very much. I used to ask what he was so happy about then. An' how comes a doctor ends up with a name like Slack? He stares at the tower block opposite as if it's Kate Moss. 'We're not here to talk about my life.' No, apparently everybody and their granny wants to talk about mine instead.

'There is order amidst the chaos', it says on one of those stupid signs in reception. Bollocks there is. There are crazies in the chaos. There are cutters and criers and catatonics in the chaos, but there's no bloody order. Still, that's what Slack says to me when he gives me the scrap book and tells me to try and find the patterns, the things that matter, the things I'd save from the fire if there was one happening in my brain like right now. I try to tell him that if there was a fire happening in my brain I'd be pretty much fucked, but he does that sighing thing he always does and looks right sad so I shrug and says 'Alright, I'll do it.'

He doesn't give me no scissors or nothing, just a pen and an exercise book, like being at school – what kind of scrap book can I make with a pen? Crap book more like. Anyways I doodled for a few pages, and it seemed to me it all might have something to do with butterflies. They was what I kept drawing anyway. Loadsa butterflies in dirty-jeans-blue Biro. There were butterfly cakes in the lounge today too. Jessica's birthday, see. I didn't think it was significant then, but now I come to think of it, there always seem to be butterflies these days. They get everywhere.

Find the patterns.

Dot-to-dot.

Hopscotch.

I drawn hundreds of butterflies while I was thinking, and they really was like those pictures I got at home, plastered on the wall instead of photographs of people – hundreds of butterflies all different shapes and wing sizes on the same page, or like stamped around this one lady's head and her, eyes shut like, but looking all complacent even though she's got all these wings flapping around her face which makes me think they must've felt nice like butterfly kisses does (you know, with eyelashes), sort of tickles, but then I thought of lots of them flapping all around me and my skin started to crawl and some had got inside my stomach flapping about and I had to take a break from the scrapbook and have a cigarette or ten, calm down like.

Jessica's birthday. Celebrating the day she arrived into the world. *A baby*. I tried to imagine Jessica all little and hairless and sucking on her dummy, shitting her pants, and I can't see that much difference to her now, sucking on that endless supply of lollipops like she's doing adverts for Chupa Chups, and wearing Tena Lady on account she's always getting a bit too excited for her bladder. She's about the same. Except she's upright, propped in an armchair with a party hat strapped under her chin. Babies when they are small are like caterpillars really, aren't they? Trying to move, crawling on their bellies in their Babygros; all-in-ones in greens and yellows and pinks, looking up at adults who look like big flowers up in the sky above them. 'Caterpillars' wriggling through the lounge with vases of chrysanthemums big like jungles and everything scary and pot plants like trees or something and cats like tigers and lions and well. God! No wonder they's always crying and bawling, babies. You would wouldn't you?

So I'm finding the patterns, well trying to any rate. Drawing the line through the maze zig-zag-zig but I get stuck on all the eyes. Like when they call you in to sit on the chair in the room and they ask you 'How are you feeling? No. Really feeling...?', not just Slack, like ALL OF THEM AT ONCE and you really have to rack your brain for something to say. Something that means they might leave you alone for five minutes. And all you can think of is their eyes, this wall of eyes watching you. Like when I shared a room with my kid brother growing up, before we moved to the Slightly Bigger Place, and he had all these pictures up on his wall, and I did too for a bit, like posters from films and stuff. All I could see was these eyes watching me from the walls and I got to thinking they might be like those paintings you see on TV drama like Mam watches all time, with old mansions and stuff where there are real people trapped in the walls or watching you or something and that's when I stopped being able to sleep. Even when I ripped them all down and got a right bollocking off Mam for it, even then I could still see the eyes like, where they *had* been.

His eyes were always there too: Peter's. Too small and dark, they were, like a rat's. Looking down at me from his big head, sweating and moaning over me. He was more like a tree than a flower, wrinkled up like bark. I had to look past them eyes, that bark. I had to look further. To the window and the sound of traffic, way down below, rushing along like a tsunami past the other tower blocks with dirty windows that you couldn't see into properly. Once there was a butterfly, right there on the glass pane. The plainest kind. A cabbage white. It looked so peaceful, so quiet. I zoned my thoughts onto it so well when I next looked up I felt lighter and he'd gone. The traffic seemed to hush and next thing the front door banged and I could hear Mam crashing pots about ready for dinner an' my brother, telling her some story about football practice and 'back of the net'. A song on the radio.

All them eyes, back in the assessment room, they turn away from me for a bit and then they brings in the caterpillar. That is how he seemed to me, see, crawling along on his belly all green and wriggly and slime trails the same green coming from his nose and joining with the spittle at his mouth. Bug-like. Not human. And caterpillars, they can fend for themselves can't they? Just need some leaves and stuff. Maybe some vegetables, like *The Hungry Caterpillar* book, see. The way I seen it, if he is a caterpillar, I surely must be a butterfly by now – I'm logical, me – and so I tried to use my wings. Flap flap. But well now they is bouncing him about in their arms and on their knees and trying to get me to hold him, and him making all that noise all the time so that I got my wings on my ears and the times I've not got my wings on my ears I'm asking why they brought the caterpillar inside when everyone knows caterpillars should be outside in the garden or down the farm crawling and eating, crawling and eating HUNGRY like in the book. Why didn't they leave him out there, where he belonged. Out there. Not with me. Nothing to do with me. Fly away Peter. Fly away Paul. Flap flap.

They keep asking the same questions when they come, whether it's Slack or the nurse or all of them. Mostly I don't say anything to them, which I s'pose is why they keep on coming back but I'm still kind of mad at myself cos way I see it I failed. All I did was flap my wings and try and fly. I ran up to the edge like a plane on a runway and jumped. Flap flap. Flap flap. Went my wings. Down, down. Down, down. Went I. They found me, anyway, so it's not like they don't know what I done or nothing is it? They's probably just having a right laugh at me, you know like with a good story when you is all 'tell me again' and then wriggling round the floor all giggling, stupid-like. Tears streaming down your face. So happy it hurts. Can't see why they can't just leave me to learn to fly and put the caterpillar back where they found him. Is them that makes no sense. Not me.

Mam's been to see me. She don't seem to have nothing to say, she just hugs me, like clamps her arms around me right tight so I can't breathe and then she lets go real quick like and pushes me away a bit, and then she leaves. Sometimes she chats to Slack out in the corridor and sometimes she don't. Peter's not been in. He stopped coming home when my belly started swelling up. Before I got bigger and bigger like strawberry bubblegum ready to pop. 'Ah, butterfly. Time to go. Fly away Peter.' He hooked his thumbs together. 'Flap flap,' Peter – Mam's boyfriend – said. 'Flap flap.' It made me giggle. It was night time. He'd used to say it when I was right small. Tickling me at bathtime. Grabbing my ankles and holding them apart, flapping them open and shut like wings. Flap flap. This time he just did the hands, made butterfly shadows go dancing across the wall, and then took his bags out to the car and left. Mam was on shift. It took her a few days to work out he'd gone. They were owls and larks work-wise, never usually saw each other in the week. Never did now neither.

'Samantha?'

I sees Slack coming towards me. I knows what look he is

wearing too. That one where he raises an eyebrow and tries to look amused and concerned and all because I'm stood bouncing on the bed with my wings out. 'Disturbing the others,' he'll no doubts call it. 'Getting them all excitable.' He's one to talk. I saw him getting them all dancing in the common room earlier. I mean, isn't that why I'd gone back up to my bed in the first place? For some peace and quiet, to think, like he said. But I unclenched my fists anyways and stopped my bouncing. The ripped-up pages of my scrapbook flutter from my hands – my paper wings hover, and then fall, crash-landing – and I, too, lose my balance.

Tap-tap. Slack's finger is at his temple. Flap-flap. Two pills fly from a plastic pot into my hand. 'Let's try these for now, eh, Samantha? Help with the turbulence. Give you a smoother flight. Okay. Will you do that? Just for me?' I try to tell him that I'm pretty much done with flying now, for today, but he does that sighing thing he always does and looks right sad so I shrug and says 'Alright.'

Dreams, Inconsistent Angel Things

'Be not inhospitable to strangers lest they be
angels in disguise' – George Whitman

Henry shut the office door, removed his glasses and began to cry. His whole body shook as the salty tears caught in the corners of his mouth before bouncing down his dirty blond beard. Not again. Nearly a year had passed and nothing, not a word; and then this. What was she playing at, interrupting his tutorial earlier? Surely she'd had her fun with him by now?

'Sorry! I guess this is the wrong room,' she'd sung, and then walked out of his life again, faded away. He rubbed at his eyes and replaced his thick-rimmed glasses, searched for his cigarettes. Retrieving them from under another pile of crumpled papers he lit one up, and stared blankly at the clutter of neglected work. There was no way he was going to tackle any of it today. Not now. His aerial view over campus revealed it to be deserted – Wednesday afternoon – sports and student slacking. Perfect all day drinking opportunities. Not such a bad idea. He opened the filing cabinet and looked for his Friday whisky supply. The bottle was virtually empty. Tipping the last lonely drops into his tepid, vending machine coffee, Henry decided on a new plan of action. The pub. If he picked the right one she might even be there, hitting bored barflies for drinks, throwing her pretty head back in fake laughter at their poor jokes. No, Henry realised, he never could plot her movements; they changed with the wind. Instead he decided he would just set off in a random direction, not the sea obviously, and stop at the first pub he came to. He heard her clap with glee, 'A decision, Oddbod, well done!' A memory giggled in his head. A drink was definitely needed.

Sweeping up his tweed jacket, Henry clambered over the ramshackle piles of unread books and journals and out of the doorway through which she had made her first, dramatic entrance. She was not one of his students, she wasn't even at the university, but a student who worked at one of the bars that she frequented had told her how his department, Psychology, always had experiments going on, and that they'd bribe you with chocolate, beer or, in this case, twenty-five quid and a free meal to take part. Not unusually for her, she was broke at the time, between benefactors. She'd turned up at Henry's office by mistake. Unlike most students she had barged in at 5.05 p.m. on a Friday as he was pouring his second whisky and, instead of explaining herself, had simply said 'Thanks!' and gulped greedily from the bottle.

Henry was not used to such intrusions, and he'd certainly not met anyone like her before. Across those crowded first week, first term freshers' lectures, perhaps, before eighty per cent dropped the class, but not up close, not actually in his world. He was unable to object, or to say anything at all. His mouth had opened and closed soundlessly as he tried to identify her. Her short hair was dyed bright turquoise and stuck out on either side of her head in stunted bunches. She was twenty or so, and had worn some kind of nightdress over a mishmash of other vibrant garments, and what looked like fuchsia pixie boots. She had showered the air in glitter with each exaggerated gesture and there was something girlishly fairytale about her, an innocence that demanded taking care of. 'So when and where do you want me?' she had asked coquettishly, before continuing, 'Soon I hope, because between you and me I could do with the cash like.' Henry coughed, flummoxed, but said nothing. She wrinkled her nose, 'You don't look like a PhD student...' She had leaned forward, throwing a wave of vanilla perfume over him as she grabbed an essay off his desk. '... *Professor* Henry Robbins,' she shrugged. 'I guess today isn't payday then.' Tilting her head to the left, and then the right, she had looked right into his eyes, and then smiled. A new plan formed. Tucking the bottle in her bag, she had poured what was left of his glass down her neck and grabbed his hand, pulling him out of his seat: 'Come on, it's Friday night, and you and I are going out.'

'Out' had meant a sprawling stumble of shots in Swansea bars. Henry had allowed himself to be swept along, a bug-eyed child on her merry-go-round, dizzied by both her attention and the excess of alcohol. The ride had whisked them through a haze of old men's pubs and cheap chain bars, where they had downed a kaleidoscope of drinks. As the bells chimed 'Last Orders!' they had moved on to a cramped, smoky speakeasy where his date had sat atop the piano and sung ethereally with a band of troubadours, before stopping, bored, mid-song, and sliding back to earth and out into the night. There, together, they had rolled down hills towards the bay, destined for a party.

Coloured fairy lights had flashed around the wide-open Bryn Road front door from which a heavy bass line thumped. Silhouettes had shape-shifted within the dimly lit interior. Miss Blue Hair had floated up the stairs above the untidy throng and Henry soared behind her. They had emerged on

73

the roof, Swansea Bay stretching out before them beneath the flickering disco lights of the stars. Around and around they spun, the city blurring below. Henry could focus on nothing but her face flying in front of him, giddily breathless, freakishly beautiful. She had called herself Pixie. To Henry this had seemed an appropriate moniker.

*

'Morning, Oddbod!'

Henry had smelt the fresh coffee as it was placed to his right. He'd attempted to open his eyes, immediately wincing at daylight. His head felt as if the local drum circle had taken up residence; all bang-bang-banging away in the name of spirituality. His spirit had ached. His spirit had wanted them to stop. Then a soft hand pushed the hair from his face. Henry had rolled over and squinted.

'There's a Pixie in your bed,' the owner of the hand had told him, brushing his cheek with her lips. Her unearthly figure had slowly come into focus.

'Headache?'

Henry nodded and gratefully swallowed the two painkillers she had given to him.

'What time is it?' He croaked. He really had felt awful.

'Picnic time – have a shower and meet me in the garden.'

He had groaned but found his body moving, obeying.

*

Feeling ever-so-slightly more human after a wash and coffee, Henry had meandered down the haphazard stairs to his narrow back garden where Pixie was dozing. She shared the guest room blanket with an array of food from the corner shop – pink wafer biscuits, tinned peaches, Greek yoghurt, French bread, dodgy-looking hummus and overpriced olives. She had opened her eyes and smiled up at his awkward, gangly frame.

'There you are Oddbod! Are you hungry? It tastes far better than it looks...'

Henry was famished; he had arranged his limbs on the blanket beside her and reached for the olives. Pixie curled around him like a cat and fell back into gentle sleep. She ended up staying with him all weekend. She neither asked nor told him that she would, but then Henry had not objected to her presence, not one little bit. They had gone charity shopping, buying obscure scratchy vinyl to play while reading aloud from the Sunday papers, and jigsaw puzzles with pieces missing to be attempted while wrapped in blankets by the bare fireplace.

From that point on, Henry found that he would often return from work to see Pixie sat, cross-legged and smoking, on the wall in front of his house. She'd seem both pleased and surprised to see him park up, hunched over the wheel of his dented old Mini. Some weeks she would appear only once, if at all. Others she would be waiting for him every night but whenever he'd offered to cut her a key she'd ignored him, pretending to search through her bottomless bag, or changing the subject. He never knew where she went those days or weeks she disappeared, but he had soon learned to stop asking. He'd become accustomed to having her around a lot of the time. Henry had felt lucky – he was, after all, middle-aged, badly dressed and lonely. He had never been good with girls, as a teenager he had been too slow to realise when he was being flirted with. Now, when he saw a student gaze coyly at him in tutorials he pretended not to notice. He thought he knew better than to make the clumsy mistakes of his suspended colleague, Griffiths. Truth-be-told he simply hadn't a clue where to start. Any women that had made an imprint in his life, and there were very few, had all made that crucial first move, and also the decision to leave. Henry had tended to go with the flow, irritatingly indecisive; he left those important choices to others. Mostly, pre-Pixie, Henry had led an inconsequential life of few surprises.

*

At first, Henry had assumed that Pixie didn't work, or that if she did it would be at a bistro, bar or theatre – something suitably 'bohemian' – but he discovered that that wasn't the case at all. 'Why would I want to work somewhere that I like to play?' she'd exclaimed. He discovered that Pixie was always walking out of her new jobs. He'd drop her off at one fresh start after another. Her reasons for the change ranged from not liking the colour of the shop walls to the sheer tedium she found herself expected to carry out each day. Filling in mindless, never-ending Excel forms for IT firms. Shredding university files in the Academic Registry. Filing pay queries in Finance. 'The work is sooooooo easy,' she'd complain. 'If they would just let me be the rest of the time, instead of making me have to pretend to be busy for all eight hours when I had clearly finished everything in two. It is too dreary. I fear I may soon turn as grey as them.' Mostly it was the routine she had hated, someone else telling her where she should be and when each day. She would say she had to pop to the bank or the dentist's and not come back, instead racing to the beach to scream at the sea; to cartwheel in the rain.

Sometimes Pixie would show up at university, gliding into the back of his lectures, appearing to listen intently. With her there in his audience Henry had found he upped his game. He had shaken himself out of his mastered monotone, raised up to his full height and spoken animatedly, fevered. She used to wait until everyone else had left at the end and applaud. 'Bravo, Oddbod, Bravo!' blowing kisses as she exited stage right. His student attendance records had improved, as had the essays he marked. Work had become less of a chore.

On the evenings that Henry came home to find Pixie waiting for him, he had cooked. Rattling pans around while she tuned his guitar and hesitantly sang old jazz numbers or, occasionally, the haunting folk songs that had made him wonder about all she kept hidden from him. When she went away was she chasing rainbows or dodging showers? He'd serve up warming bowls of dhal or pasta and watch her wolf the food down as if she hadn't eaten since she last visited; which dawned upon him as entirely possible. Some nights he'd found her sat on his wall drinking wine from the bottle, eyes shining. Others she'd dragged him out to join pub quizzes halfway through, to stand and watch bands play in darkened rooms, to down more than their fair share of free chardonnay at art openings and book launches. She had instructed him to lie on the floor looking up at gallery installations – ceilings covered in ping pong balls, glowing red, or seals gliding across glacial blue screens. 'Look how free they are!' she'd exclaimed in wonderment. In return he had shared scraps of related facts he had garnered from books and long forgotten classes on art history. He only told her the juiciest snippets, the quirkiest stories, but often she would look pleased. Sometimes she would even ask him to repeat what he had said, scribbling it down in her tatty notebook. It was rare that she would stifle a yawn, and say 'Yes, Professor' before shutting him up with kisses.

They seldom went to the same place together twice, and yet people would nod at her in recognition and eye him with idle curiosity as they sent drinks her way. He had enjoyed their outings and the admiring glances Pixie received, yet she always seemed restless, fidgeting, uncertain that they were in the best possible location. Perhaps they should have done this or gone there instead. She was rarely this way at his house, he'd noticed; there she had appeared completely at ease, often lost in her dreams. He had only seen her this comfortable in two other places – the beach and the botanical gardens. Racing out of the sea, with bronzing summer skin and salted hair, or strolling along the tide line as she searched for pretty shells and other treasures; finding magic among the flotsam and jetsam, and spinning tales. Henry would sit on the dunes and pretend to read, watching Pixie acting completely at home, half expecting her to morph into a mermaid and leave him for the ocean with a flick of her scaly tail. He knew he had fallen in love.

Pixie had been hanging around Henry for six months when he found himself saying the words. 'Marry me?' They had taken their breakfast to the botanical gardens in Singleton Park en route to his 11 a.m. class. Pixie had been chattering ten to the dozen among the brightly coloured blooms in the humid, tropical greenhouses. His words were left hanging in the frosted morning air outside. She had shrugged, pulled her bag onto her shoulder and then wordlessly retreated to her latest job, sorting web orders in the damp, dark basement of a music store. He had kicked himself.

*

The house had looked different as Henry approached it, silent, solemn. The wall outside lay bereft of a Pixie. It had been eight days since his proposal and the longest she had ever left it between visits. His essays had all been marked, his lectures planned well in advance, the *Guardian* crosswords completed. He had begun passing his evenings pacing the length of the living room, fingering the strings of his guitar, thinking of her, waiting for her. Nothing. She hadn't written. She hadn't called. Every night he had returned hoping to find her sat outside, or to see the new message light flashing on his answer phone. It scarcely ever did, and the disappointment to hear his mother or his bank instead of her light voice pained him. He should have known better than to force her into a corner like that. Where was she?

He had tried the bars they'd drunk in to no avail, regulars and bar staff all feigned ignorance. 'Who?' 'Pixie? No mate, seen a few fairies in my time though.' Ha ha ha. Henry had persisted, and he must have had a drink in each place he looked because he had repeatedly found himself escorted off various premises by the burly arms of bouncers, their eyes filled with pity. He had thought of her eyes, the way she looked right to his core, how they stripped him defenceless, how they charmed. He had tried to be logical in his search. He scrawled lists and realised how little he knew of the facts of her life. All he had left of her was ephemera – bus tickets, lunch notes and doodles. He had never been to see where she lived; he didn't even have an address for her. Did she even have a home? He didn't know any of her family; she never ever spoke of them, or of her home town, or the names of her closest friends. He had tried the places she'd claimed to work, but met with brick walls at each one. It occurred to him that he had never dropped her to the door of an office, or tried to visit her at a job. The intricate web of lies she appeared to have fed him intrigued Henry even more. Christ! He didn't even know her real name!

Though he thought that he knew the city well, Henry had bought maps of Swansea and marked all the places they had visited together. He had searched the house high and low for a photo of her although he knew there were none but the ones on permanent slideshow in his mind. Lying amidst daisies in Cwmdonkin Park. Excited, stood beside the giant snow bunny they had made in February, in her tea cosy hat, cheeks rosy from the cold. In bed, innocent when she dreamt. Outside,

Henry saw her everywhere and yet nowhere. She was walking through Uplands, her hair hidden by an umbrella. She was a laugh tinkling down the corridor that sent him running down eight flights of stairs, arriving sweaty, red-faced and panting on the deserted ground floor. She was an apparition, his own personal mirage greeting him on his doorstep, fading as he stepped forward to embrace her. He didn't sleep. He couldn't sleep. He missed her cold feet burying under him, each toenail messily coated in blue varnish. He missed her talk.

After two weeks panic began to set in. Henry had roamed the city night after night hoping to stumble upon her at this bar or that. He had left notes to her in the gardens and tacked to park benches under a wide-eyed moon. He even considered going to the police, but what could he say?

'Excuse me officer, a young girl I know has disappeared.'

'Yes, sir, and what is her name?'

'Pixie.'

'Her full name, sir, if you please.'

'I don't know.'

'And where does she live? Do you know the address?'

'Erm, well mostly with me.'

They would look him over with a mixture of pity and suspicion. They'd either listen to his description of her, smell the booze on his breath, his clothes, and laugh. Tell him that they thought, perhaps, that he had simply been dumped. They would joke about it at home after dinner with the missus or down the pub with their mates. Or worse still, they would take him for crazy. Believe he had murdered her. Probably dig up his garden. Lock him in prison and throw away the key. He sighed. No, there was no point in telling them.

Pixie had seemed so free when she walked into his office, and in those first few months afterwards, and yet later she had made herself his caged bird for a while. The blue hair had grown out to white blonde as she'd busied her days with sporadic temp jobs and making his garden grow, nursing the sick yellow roses back to life, her chipped nails permanently ingrained with soil. Despite her own diluting palette she had seemed happy. They had laughed and they had talked. They had made love, and slowly they had even begun to make plans. While Pixie had sat sewing new bedroom curtains and burning heady, scented candles, Henry's thoughts had turned to a wedding. He was old-fashioned, he believed love and marriage went together, but expressing this to Pixie had made her scared and fugitive. She had effectively feathered their nest and then flown it.

He could still list all the places beginning with 'P' that she wanted to visit: Patagonia, Paraguay, Peru, Penzance, Pirate Ships, and Prague at sunrise. His head filled with things that he knew of her. Favourite colour – Green. Favourite number – 'Five!' said with the fingers of one hand splayed in front of her face. Favourite flowers – sweet peas. She liked Billie Holiday not Peggy Lee. Pasta not rice. The radio over TV. The left side of the bed. Marmite. She hadn't the patience to read many books and she didn't like films. 'What use are other people's stories?' she'd say. 'Life is for your own living.' Despite this, she encouraged him to write papers and attend talks, to further his academic career. Mostly she encouraged him in the art of living. He remembered her trying to teach him to cartwheel in Gower during a thunderstorm at Caswell. He could still taste the mouthful of sand as he collapsed again and again; still hear their laughter slamming together, relentlessly. He could still see her writhing on the wet ground in stitches. The play fights with handfuls of kelp.

The weeks of Pixie's absence had become months and Henry suffered from the lack of her. He had stopped shaving, the initial bristle of stubble had grown into a full beard and his unkempt, uncut hair fell in his blue-grey eyes as he mumbled his way, barely conscious, through his lectures on sleep, memory and perception. He had stopped listening out for the telltale creak of the lecture theatre's back door. The monotone was back, as was the slouch. Attendance (his and that of his students) had fallen below par. Final exams had come and gone, and the empty void of the summer holidays stretched out before him like a jail sentence. Henry had thought back to the summer before; of camping at Three Cliffs and blazing bonfires throwing dancing light onto their chatty, animated faces late into the night. He had hoped that Pixie just needed some time. He'd hoped that she would return to him but she had not. There had been neither sightings nor word. Now he passed his long, lonely days walking and drinking, sometimes thinking he'd found something of her at the bottom of a bottle, falling down when he reached out to touch her.

*

'Sorry! I guess this is the wrong room.' Pixie's voice was back in his head. Damn her! Many months had passed and yet Henry could now smell that familiar, cheap vanilla scent everywhere he went. He could feel her head resting on his chest, her arms looped around him, and yet she was not there with him. He felt as dizzy as that first night they had spent out together, dancing high upon the rooftops. He had to pause and catch his breath, steadying himself on a lamppost, breathing slowly. He thought of her intrusion earlier. How, instantly recognising her singsong voice, he'd swung round, dislodging his glasses and squinting at the figure disappearing out of his half-open door. He couldn't speak or focus fast enough. Righting his specs he had excused himself from his new semester of students and scanned the dimly lit corridor. Empty. Concentrating, he'd heard the heavy creak of the fire door as it had scraped along the standard issue carpet – the colour of spilt black coffee – to the stairwell and boxy lift. Henry had raced around the corner and, wheezing, had swung through the doors just as the lift closed and the carriage had begun its treacherous descent to the ground floor.

'Damn it.' Henry had sunk into a nearby plastic chair. He closed his eyes, pained, and brought his hand to his forehead – he remained silent in this position for a while before returning to dismiss his class early. His heart was still racing as he strolled to the pub and old conversations replayed through his mind. 'Do you think we could live like this forever?' she'd slurred once, lolling against him as they made their way home from a long drinking session. 'You know, together and happy. You and me?' 'Forever and a day,' he'd replied. They'd never spoke of it, although he had thought of it often. He had reached The Cricketers, a pub large enough to make his solo drinking more anonymous and bearable. There, where the jukebox and television battled it out against the kitchen banter to see which could be the most annoying noise, he ordered a pint of Guinness and found some solace in the tumbledown beer garden.

He remembered doing the quiz with Pixie there one random Thursday. He'd driven over to meet her for just one pint, but as usual one was never enough. She'd widened her glittered gaze at him as he'd made his shuffle to leave, 'Oh come on, Oddbod, the bar is that-away, mine's a Worthy's.' Then a large man in a loud shirt had waddled over and informed them that his music quiz was about to start and at Pixie's insistence they'd paid their fifty pence and failed badly. The songs were before Pixie's time, but not retro cool enough for her to know them. The couple of answers he had known he'd kept to himself for fear of Pixie's riling. She'd got fed up way before halfway through, yawning theatrically and dragging him somewhere else. He realises he can't remember where, though he probably, foolishly, drove there.

Despite himself, the extent to which he missed her troublesome, demanding ways and her gentler affection had not diminished with time. So much time had dropped out of sight, like she had, melted away.

His pint was not having the desired, dulling effect. Henry ordered a Stella instead, hoping the wife-beating bubbles might unclog his muddled mind. He reached for another cigarette and realised he had already chain-smoked the pack he'd bought en route. This was not good. He fumbled with a handful of coins at the machine. Returning to his seat he opened the packet, placed one in his mouth and searched his pocket for a lighter.

Someone beat him to it.

Dainty arms encircled him, sparking his cigarette up from behind.

Henry looked at the small hand, the bitten-down fingernails and chipped blue varnish. The gossamer skin. The garish rings.

Enclosing those fine fingers in his spare hand, he kissed them slowly, one by one, and then turned around.

Stung

At the moment, right this very minute, I am having a battle of wills with a wasp. Me – a grown woman – at war with a tiny little insect. It is winter again. It always seems to be winter these days. This morning I was doing my weekly online grocery shop when, all of a sudden, I heard a buzz in the paper lightshade above me. I saw the ominous flash of black and yellow flitting about inside the white globe and had to decamp from the cosy comfort of the sofa and hide in the bedroom. I ran, in truth. Legged it. Now, four hours, thirty-three minutes and seventeen seconds later, we are at a stand-off.

In my head we have a psychic understanding – one open-plan living space, two living beings minding their own – and if Waspy sticks to it then I won't have to murder her. She is in the kitchen now, buzzing around the other big bulb, and I am squinting in the lamplight, back in the lounge. Tactics. I figure the waspish one can stay put until she kills herself headbutting objects, or until morning when I fling open all of the windows and hide the cake. Until then she can hover over there and I'll attempt to settle over here; our harmonious, if divided, territories.

Buzz.

Even this far away I can still hear her, the noisy cow. I mean, wasp. I've had to put some music on to drown her out. I have some other distractions – a herbal tea for my nerves and a book for my eyes. At school and even at work these days we are always told to ignore the bullies and they will go away. I am trying that tactic, but even though my survival strategies are in place I still can't quite get the idea of the sting out of my head. Bees I could handle, bees only kill when they have to; wasps, in my opinion, are mean.

I don't have a friend to phone so I asked the audience of WikiAnswers what I should do instead. They seemed confused. Wasps are meant to be dead or hibernating at this time of year. I skim read the reams of screen and find what I am looking for. I don't like it. The oracle basically informs me that this wasp is most likely to be a queen looking to hibernate, as she tends to outlive her nest and flee it. If fills me with doom to discover that if it is a queen, she could decide to make a nest in the flat, and thousands more wasps will be hatching here in the summer. Eek! I hardly dare read on but I do. If it is not a queen, then she is a *he*, a worker on his last legs, and hence a male with nothing to lose but his sting. Despite my irrational fear I brave a trip to the kitchen. I need to know. I think that she is a female, although the sluggish one-too-many-sugars stagger does remind me of one or two men from my past, lying prostrate on the pavement outside my door with big goofy love-me grins, holding a kebab akimbo. Their house keys lost, any sense of time or sobriety lost, along with any chance of maintaining an erection, or of sleeping in the bed that night.

Buzz.

Even with memories like that, I still abhor living alone on days like this. It would be nice, more than nice, to have someone else to deal with things like wasps, trip switches and my broadband provider. To hold my hand. I have, through the varying hovels of my life, been forced to learn to cope with most bugs: spiders – except those the size of a small child – and even cockroaches and mice I can deal with, but wasps still freak me out. My heart is thumping. I want to leave – not just the room, but the house. I'm afraid of the sting in their tail and I hate the way they turn on you, creep up in beer gardens and steal your boozy nectar before attacking you for your benevolence. It's just not polite.

The last time I saw a wasp, at least that I can remember, before tonight, was in high summer. I was on a date, a snatched afternoon in the country on my way to a job. A cool pint on a hot day, a riverbank, some mountains and us. Invading, swarming into our idyllic moment were – in equal supply – wasps and German hikers. When the first wasp edged onto our table I moved my drink and myself closer to my date and we kissed. When the second came dizzily circling, I jumped, and when the third arrived I ran, screaming like a banshee, tears streaming from my eyes. Unreasonable, phobic reactions. The hikers briefly looked up from studying their maps and shook their heads before returning to plotting, folding and unfolding. My date caught my eye and raised his monobrow. I shrugged as he came over to me, and he ruffled my hair.

'You're actually really scared?'

I nodded.

He patted me on the shoulder and returned to our table where he made noble and gallant gestures, trapping wasps under glasses. It was a battle he could not win; each angry imprisoned wasp seemed to attract more, like elephants mourning their dead. It was awkward. The situation forced us to drink up faster than we would have liked; to cut our meeting short. The relationship went the same way. Fast, troublesome and short-lived.

Buzz.

I want to leave the house but I can't. I've already left once today, and that is all I can muster at the moment. One short walk to the local shop and back every twenty-four hours, at my doctor's insistence. I buy a pint of milk and exchange pleasantries with the owners. My fridge is full of half-drunk bottles of semi-skimmed milk; curdling. I open it up and that's all I see. Often, in the shop, as I hotfoot it to the fridge and then carefully count out my change at the till, I will notice an old and papery lady, perhaps two, sat at the other end of the long counter drinking tea. They talk to the mother or the daughter of the family who run the store about their aches and pains, or show them photos of their grandchildren whom they adore but rarely have chance to visit.

I am not an old woman but sometimes I wish that I could join them there, that I could be handed a steaming cup, one custard cream, and some of the same kindness to help me on my way. That they would take my shopping list from my hand and put it all together for me while I supped and chatted. Then they could carry my bags and lead me back home in time for *The Archers*. I am not old. I am twenty-eight, and so instead I thank the man at the till and force a smile as he nods. I pick up my pint of milk and walk the three minutes and forty-two seconds back to the front door of my building. I fiddle with keys. I check the postbox in the hall – empty – before I climb up the stairs to my flat and bolt the door behind me.

Buzz.

It may not sound like much, but it is progress. After the accident I stopped going out. Not just socially; everything. The only time I would open my flat door was to put out the rubbish and check my mail. Once a week. At first I didn't feel like eating, so shopping wasn't a concern, and what with me being such a hoarder, such an impulse three-for-two buyer when I didn't even need one, it was a while before I required much of anything. Plus, seeing as how I wasn't going out, or seeing anyone, my cleaning routine – of clothes, the house, myself – was kind of falling by the wayside. Like it does when you are getting over a break-up, or a death. Like it did during the aftermath of the obliteration of my family, all three of them killed in a car crash. My mother, father and brother – gone – on the way to pick me up from dance class. The drunken seventeen-year-old at the wheel survived and was jailed. I was a year younger than him. Orphaned. My best mate's parents took me in while I studied for my A-levels. They fed me and found me a lawyer, helped with the paperwork. I filled their garage, their shed, and their attic with things from the house. They were good to me, and good to their own kids. It was too much. I left them and college six months later. I fled to the seaside – got a room of my own, and a job in a bookshop. I inherited a fair whack of cash, but it didn't feel right to spend it back then. More recently, though, it did.

When I was younger I used to live above my parents' shop. On evenings and weekends, or school holidays, when I wasn't with friends or waitressing or babysitting elsewhere, I would help out. I would put together orders, ring them through the till. When it snowed I would take what I could carry to the elderly and disabled. I would walk for three miles through the white stuff so that our local Lord and Lady weren't left short of whisky. Everybody in that village knew my name. Only a handful of people in this city do. Not one neighbour. Not even the shopkeeper. Just my GP and the nurses and doctors at the hospital, and even they will have long forgotten me in the shifts of trauma and travesty that have been and gone since.

Buzz.

It is the intercom buzzing this time, although the wasp is still alive, and still in the kitchen. My supermarket home delivery has arrived. I can see the van outside. I go downstairs. On the way to the door I consider asking the delivery person about the wasp. Upon opening the door to her scowl I think better of it. I take the bags. The woman waits impatiently for my signature, and then leaves. She doesn't say a word. After the intercom our whole conversation is carried out through gestures and nods. If I didn't sing in the shower, and buy milk from the shop, I wonder if my voice would fail me. It already squeaks sometimes, like an engine in dire need of oil.

Since I stopped going out I've taken to hanging out with my laptop. We watch films together, listen to the same music, and play against each other in games. Often it beats me. I never was that good at winning. That is why I play hearts or solitaire and not online poker, chess or war games. I would like to make other, human friends, but like I say, I don't go out. And I don't trust online identities. I don't want to befriend an eight-year-old. Or a psychopath. I know it is the digital age and everyone and their granny is plugged in and posting pictures of their drunken antics online, but somehow that doesn't make me feel any better about the whole thing. I'd rather be friends with a robot. That said, I now do almost everything else through the web. Bank stuff, shopping, video cookery lessons, the lot. I also get the papers delivered at the weekend. I read each supplement cover to cover. The columnists feel like family, bickering with each other across the dining table. They comfort me. I sit there with a pair of scissors and a highlighter. I make scrapbooks of the stories that interest me, and recycle the rest. Last week I read that bees are dying out. That in ten years they may be extinct, and then, so would we. It backed up my doomed theories about the world. About life. It should be the fate of wasps. I cut it out. I paste it in with the others.

Buzz.

I haven't always been such a pessimist. I used to be the opposite – a glass-half-full kind of girl. Even after that car crash, my family's funeral, I'd have pissed you off with my happy-go-lucky ways; I really would. I'm not sure whether I changed from bloom to gloom when the morning-after pill failed, when I made the decision to go through with the pregnancy, when my ex said 'Okay, if that's what you want, but you're on your own. I'm done,' or with the accident. I guess it doesn't matter so much. I know I wasn't an optimist on that February day when it snowed, although I was smiling for some of it. I smiled when I looked out of my window and saw snowflakes floating down – thousands of tiny frosted fallen angels dropped from a rose-tinted sky. I smiled when they stuck. I smiled when I went outside in my hat and gloves and took photos of the trees as children raced up and down the street fighting with snowballs. But I cried when I slipped and found myself lying on the floor, the snow-covered street between my legs turning the colour of cherry Slushpuppie. I cried at the hospital before they even said the word miscarriage, and I cried as I said a few words. My name. My address. That I was twenty-two weeks gone. With twins. I used to like the number two. I used to be an optimist. But things change.

I cleared the nursery last week. The Moses baskets, the toys, the Babygros and the mobiles that I had made for them both with all the colourful stars. I kept one toy and one pair of booties for each lost child. I put the rest of their things up on Freecycle.com, insisted that everything went to one person, who would take it away in one trip. Once I had chosen someone I cleaned myself up, and the flat. She was nice. The girl who came. With her big bump and a big grin that she tried, but failed, to stifle. Her husband and his friend loaded it all up into the van. I stood in the kitchen, clasping a coffee mug and a rattle. When they were done the girl came and stood in front of me and then she did the strangest thing. She hugged me. Not just a quick squeeze, either, but the way you would comfort a sad child. Then she pulled back, thanked my startled face, and waddled off. I cried again that day, for the first time since I'd left the hospital. Bu...

The buzzing is getting louder again. The light shade is no longer rattling with the drunken queen. My heart rate quickens. One would think, seeing as I haven't actually been stung by a wasp for twelve years, that I would have been able to surmount the obstacle of my phobia by now. That I wouldn't need to create battles of will with teeny tiny insects. The thing about phobias is that they rarely make any real sense. The thing about mine is that it does. On the day that my mother, my father and my younger brother were killed, they were coming to collect me from dance class. It was summer and we had been practising our routine outside, on the bouncy lawn. A wasp took a liking to the inside of my pink tracksuit bottoms, but not to my leg.

The resulting stings caused it to swell massively. My allergies are severe, but not life-threatening, so I didn't die that day. But three other people did.

Buzz.

The absconded queen lands on the coffee table in front of me and staggers around a sticky circle left by an earlier glass of pop. She has broken her end of the divided territories deal. I see red. Quite literally – the squashed result of this action is magnified through the bottom of the glass. 'I'm sorry.' I whisper it, not to the wasp but to some God I don't believe in. Outside, cars slide through the rain. A blustery wind whips smoke from the mouths of staggering drunks on the street below. It tugs at the windows, but for today winter remains outside.

ARRIVALS

a novella

'Sometimes when I tell the story of you
I make you out to be the bad guy
And though it's true
Sometimes you are the bad guy
You're still mine.'

from 'The Good & The Bad Guy'
by My Brightest Diamond

Amy

If life went the way I wanted it to, the way it did in my dreams, my journey to Los Angeles would have turned out a little differently. The stills would have been bleached out and long and lazy like those from a good road movie. I would have arrived in LA in a beat-up Chevy, with Johnny Depp circa *What's Eating Gilbert Grape* at the wheel besides me, after snaking up Route 66. Once we arrived we would have found the sepia-toned Hollywood of the 1950s or 60s – all that glitz and glamour. Stars, not 'celebs'. Instead, the lacklustre LA that greets me resembles a British enterprise park, the same soulless low-rise structures, but with wider roads and a noticeable lack of home improvement stores. My life hasn't been going my way much at all lately. Still, I should count my blessings and be grateful that my plane did not crash. I travelled by air direct from LHR to LAX where a man lay in wait for me. A man I didn't remember. A man who had been missing for my whole life, or so it felt.

On the plane I'd been strapped into an aisle seat in the middle section of first class. Next to me a like-mother-like-daughter pair ate grotesquely, shovelling the tiny portions of airline food into their big mouths with bigger hands. Fake

Chanel bling and baubles had spilled from their earlobes and choked at their flabby necks. I couldn't eat – I'd forced down one pretzel and one glass of champagne. In ten hours. I knew I should have consumed more – it being free and all – but I'd found I was too nervous to chew and swallow. Too worried about what was to come next.

The in-flight films didn't help – they all seemed to have the same themes of reunion and happy ever after. They had made me feel worse. I was not five any more, but nineteen. I didn't believe in God and I didn't believe in fairy tales. The only thing I did know happened with any surety was death. It was why I'd come to LA. I had started planning the trip after going to my first ever funeral. Turned out I had a vacancy for a man in my life and so it seemed appropriate. Although, if my mother had known where my first port of call was to be, I bet you a dollar that she wouldn't have agreed.

*

The waiting man, Allan, had met me at the airport as planned. Initially I didn't take in much; at arrivals he had stood holding an A4 sheet of paper up to the glass wall between us. The name on my passport was biro-scrawled across it. I had to look twice because I use a different moniker at home, my 'known as' name, my spy name. He was shorter than I had imagined. That had been the only thought to cross my mind before I had been caught up in passport control and baggage retrieval. Then, when I had been spat out at the other end of conveyer belts, fingerprints and form-filling, my hunger and nerves swapped places; took over. I needed to eat.

We loaded my rucksack into Allan's car. It wasn't a Chevy. He wasn't Johnny Depp. The disappointment bit. The man I didn't remember drove us past charmless motels and malls to a soundtrack of 'The Love Hour' on a soft rock radio station before pulling up at a place named Lou's Diner. There, we sat down awkwardly at an ugly plastic table, facing each other like opposing armies. I devoured the menu, and then the food when it had arrived, swiftly, while taking stealth looks at my lunch date over the sauce bottles. We ate in silence, and as we did I tried to recall something about him. Anything. All I could find were a few stored stills put to memory from curling snapshots. A bowed head of dark curls. A roman nose. A garden with an apple tree. The legs I had once sat upon going down the slide. There were no facts or quotable lines of dialogue that sprang to mind; just swatches of fabric and snatches of scenes.

A question. The real world came back into focus. I raised my tired eyes to the mouth that had spoken the words. Livery lips lying expressionless above a double chin. I raised my gaze further across the pale, overweight face to the glass-blue eyes blinking back at me through dark, stunted lashes. The face, taken in its entirety, had a ghostlike quality, like the faded photograph that I had carried in my wallet for the last nine years, found abandoned and long forgotten within a splintered box in the garage. Time had altered its shape and softened once-chiselled features to create an ageing-baby in place of a young man, the familiar contours masked by well-fed flesh. I almost reached out with my hands to wave them through what was surely an apparition; instead I pinched myself to rein in my jet lag, and I noticed the Thai waitress smiling away to my right was neither chewing gum nor called Velma. This was no stereotypical American diner. This was no typical day. Allan spoke once again, his soft English Midlands tones stretched and twisted by seventeen years of LA living.

'Do you want anything else, sugar?'

Did I want anything else? I dangled my red patent ballet pump from my bare toes as I considered the question. My thoughts rewound – zipping across the planet, and time, to a poky North London house full of black furniture, industrial chrome, and late 1980s decor highlighted with red, grey and white. Slatted Venetian blinds shuttered the windows through which the last of the afternoon sun seeped, interrupting the fuzzy picture on the TV. Upstairs a flame-haired woman – my mother, Maggie – lay in bed sobbing, unable to hush the repeated questions of her toddler daughter that crescendoed into tantrum-wet breaths of

'I want...

'I want...

'I want...

I whipped on through my mind maps to childhood aspirations and pink satin shoes. To twirling and tutus, and then toecaps – steel – turning my left foot swollen and red, then purple, then green, then yellow. A torn ligament and two bones chipped away from joints. The end of my *Swan Lake* dreams.

In the diner I paused, as if for effect, before leaning far forward; my fingers splayed across the table. I widened my eyes and whined:

'I want... an ice cream, please.'

To my surprise his face lit up and he laughed; a big-bellied laugh of relief, a freeze-breaker. It filled the whole room, causing necking couples to come up for air, startled, and jocks to turn their eyes from the game on the TV.

'Why, sure!' he bellowed, and then, quieter, to the waitress: 'Get this pretty girl whatever she wants.'

I leant back against the plastic seat of the booth and ordered the biggest sundae on the menu, unable to escape the childlike pleasure burning across my cheeks, and the anger subsiding against my will. I remembered my best friend's words at Heathrow: 'Have you considered that you might actually like the guy?' No, no, no I hadn't. I frowned, pulling my limbs up along with my defences and making my version of small talk while my long-absent biological father sipped his coffee, oblivious to his comedy work tie dipping in and out of his cooling chowder.

Sip.

I worried the bitten skin around my right thumbnail. Said-what-I-saw in touristy amusement with a poor imitation of a Californian accent: 'Jell-o. Pinball. Restroom.' And so on, as if the novelty would never wear thin.

Sip.

The smiling tea-tray returned with the sky-scraping sundae, complete with sparklers celebrating their quick-burn existence. As the last silver sparks darted across the rainbow dish I tucked in, grateful to have something to do with my mouth other than attempt to remove the awkward silence. My mind was still trying to trace my own features into those of the man in front of me. They didn't match up.

'You look like your aunt, my sister, Evelyn.' He said, suddenly, as if reading my mind. His voice cutting through the silence between us like static.

'A Picasso girl, a long-faced muse, all eyes. She was a ballet dancer. You're a beanpole like your grandpa, mind, and your uncle, your mum's side of course.' He talked with his mouth full.

I stared at him, trying to digest the words along with my food. Although stilted, it was the most he had said at once since I'd arrived. I attempted to think of something to say back but a lanky kid started playing pinball aggressively directly to my left, stealing my attention. I watched his back arch as the ball flung itself around and around the epileptic lights of the machine before a slamming finale. Game over, he swaggered back across to his perch at the counter, a cowboy mounting his horse; catching me watching him. I dropped my head, letting black curls fall over my rising blush, hoping Allan hadn't noticed. I turned my attention back to dessert, sugared reassurances glided down my throat, spoon-by-silent-spoon.

As the ice cream disappeared, the expanse between Allan and me seemed to widen accordingly, an open mouth waiting to be fed. The diner's glass door slammed regularly, marking other customers coming and going. The cash register rang, coins rattled and coffee pots steamed. Words seemed to reach our lips before thinking better of escaping.

'You know, I'm pretty tired.' I said finally, and bit my lower lip.

Allan looked disappointed, and then checked his expression with a broad smile that didn't reach his eyes.

'Yes, of course, you must be, I'll drop you at the hotel.' He spoke slowly, as if chewing each word, before rising abruptly and paying our tab.

*

At the hotel we said our farewells like a teenage couple ejecting themselves from a bad date. I felt like I needed to do something to rectify the moment but I couldn't work out what.

'So I'll see you tomorrow?' I offered shyly, uncertain.

'Yes, I'll ring after breakfast, or ring me when you're up?' his voice a whisper.

'Okay.' I nodded more than necessary, gathering up my bags from the back seat, opening up the car door. Then, suddenly, like an Olympic hurdler, he was out of the car and at my side – short arms hugging me; a quick, wet peck on the cheek – a better ending for our first date.

'Goodnight then.'

'Night.'

My car door banged shut, and I was stopped from turning, leaving the scene, by the briefest flash of terror that raced across Allan's face. I followed his gaze to the car. A second-hand silver five-door Ford. A family car. The engine was still running. He tried my door. Locked. I began to mutter:

'Oh no no no. Oh no.'

Then quieter still, 'Oh fuck!'

I took in the keys – still in the ignition – and all the doors with the central lock down. Locked tight, childproof. I started to laugh. The valet boys looked over in mild interest.

The car was parked right by the hotel's busy main entrance.

Allan brought his hand to his face, 'My spare keys are in the trunk!' A goofy smile brightened his features, along with the faint blush of embarrassment.

'Your bag must have knocked the central lock.' His tone was matter-of-fact, not accusatory.

'The engine's still running.' I stated the obvious. Then, sinking under the full weight of my travel exhaustion, 'I'm sorry, God, I'm really sorry.'

Allan circled the car trying all the doors. A bellboy wheeling a rail of garments to the car in front caught his eye. 'Problem?'

I yawned, and rubbed at my eyes.

'It's my fault, absolutely, I locked him out.'

'You got spare keys?'

'In the trunk.'

'You got cover?' He raised an eyebrow.

'No.' Allan shoe-gazed apologetically.

The bellboy exhaled a long, low whistle and then a chuckle. He called two of the valet parkers over. A little crowd encircled the two of us, our mild embarrassment turning from tickled-pink to alarm-red. The same questions were asked. Allan kicked at the exhaust in a now-irritated attempt to stall the engine, it failed. Old Ford keys were dug out and tried; apparently it was a common design flaw. None of the staff seemed eager to show that they could break into cars. This was an honest job with the promise of big tippers. They sighed and tutted loudly. The car was in the way at primetime at the hotel; hipsters were drifting off to mark out their place in life in the bars of Santa Monica and Beverly Hills. In their wake, sleep-hungry suits crawled back from long dinner meetings to prepare presentations and place long-distance duty calls home before pushing a glass or four around the bar until bed.

One of the locks, the back door behind the driver's, looked raised.

'Is that open?'

'No, it just looks that way.'

'Maybe we can hook that...'

Doorstops were brought out from the lobby to try to force a gap in the window. Broken aerials were used to fish at the keys, the locks. No luck. Elbows and angles entangled. The more they failed, the greater the determination appeared knitted into the men's sweaty brows. My eyelids drooped, I swayed ever so slightly, no longer able to take in the lessons of car-jacking.

'Go on up, there's nothing you can do...' Allan suggested, resigned to a long night.

'I know, I will in a bit...'

Wherever I stood appeared to be where the action was needed. After half an hour of faffing, I caved in to Allan's suggestion. I had just located my favourite oversized sleep T-shirt in the bottom of my badly packed rucksack as the phone rang in my room.

'Just to let you know that they did it, some obscure combination of luck and persistence and a trusty coat hanger. I'm on my way home, finally. See you tomorrow, don't call too early, I think we both need some rest.'

*

I awoke from heavy sleep tangled in white sheets, pillows strewn across the floor, the engine-whirr of planes at close range overhead. My surroundings became more familiar with rising consciousness, like the sun burning off a morning fog. The radio alarm clock to my right blinked at 07:15. Early. I opened the curtains and stood at the window, considering the clear blue sky into which planes were taking off and landing at the airport across the way, like young birds testing their wings for the first time. It was already warm. I turned the air con up and flicked the TV on to a kids' channel then showered, the surging bolts of hot water unclogging stubborn mascara remains, stinging my eyes. Harsh hotel toiletries stripped my hair and skin of moisture, leaving me clean yet sandpaper dry, abrasive.

'Not too early.' Allan's words resounded in my head as I made coffee and pulled on a vintage sixties shift dress. I roughly dried my tangled hair with a white towel, leaving a tell-tale trail of blue-black dye like dirty tears. I'd forgotten to pack an adaptor plug and the room-issued, asthmatic hairdryer wheezed out a barely tangible trickle of cool air. I gave up on it, instead scraping the length of it back and fastening the bulk into a loose knot at the nape of my neck. A messily heavy ring of kohl encircled each startled eye. I knocked back the now lukewarm coffee and wandered down to breakfast – a giant bowl of granola, berries and yoghurt and an endless supply of coffee, at least until serving time ended. I wasn't usually one for morning eating but the evasive nature of hours in transatlantic travel had left my body even more confused than usual. Everything felt dreamlike although I knew I really was there, in the USA, and the farthest I'd ever been from home. There were those nerves again, causing goosebumps to rise in ridges along both arms. I cupped my hands around my filter coffee, drawing the heat to my palms.

This wasn't my first trip abroad, I'd picked fruit and flowers in Ireland and France, and danced in fields and deserts at festivals across Europe from Somerset to Spain, but this trip was The Big One, and not only because of The Father Thing. Destination Numero Uno was top secret and had been skipped from the itinerary I had shown mum before I left. The one posted up on my travel blog. She thought that I was trailing the beats in San Francisco, like I had always wanted to do, like she had always wanted to do too. Most of the garishly dressed, face-painted kids I had played games with on long summer afternoons – the offspring of my mother's liberal friends – had since sought rules and structure in their worlds, opting for careers in the army or police force, or they were grade A students headed for teaching, law or medicine. The rest – the 'creatives' – liked to spend their days cloaked in a perpetual darkness; encased in heady, fog-filled living rooms where sarong-covered windows kept out daylight and later streetlights. The Wii gave way to a buzzing black and white snowstorm on the box in the corner while YouTube antics gathered chuckles from another. Multiple bodies spilled across carpets and grubby sofas, among upturned ashtrays and empty cider bottles, all under a haze of pot-smoke and incense. But while I had opted for lizard lounging, I had felt I belonged to neither group. I lived in a world with the edges softened and blurred and yet something inside me had niggled, an itch demanding scratching. I had wanted more but I couldn't define what that meant. I hadn't expected the phone call.

*

'Amy?'

The faltering female voice on the other end was high-pitched, and followed by a sob. It was Naomi, one of my closest friends. She explained that my ex-boyfriend had now dumped not just me, but also the world. He had been run over, hit while walking the wrong way down the centre of the North Circular ranting and raving, speed psychosis. Dead and gone.

'Dan.' I'd repeated his name softly into the void as the receiver went dead.

*

I'd worn a sunshine yellow dress to the funeral. Dan's mother had told me to get everyone to wear colour. To celebrate his life. It felt clichéd but I still told people to tell people. I guess they thought I was mad crazy with bereavement or something, as they disobeyed. Instead, when our mates showed up they formed a sea of drab; dull as hell. Mum had wilted in rose pink, welling up whenever she looked at me, as if I were going to spend my life as a Miss Havisham clone. The place was packed. The first gaudy rows of his family clashed and hurt my tear-scored eyes. There were the people who cared, who had a right to be there – friends of Dan's, his family, and the like – and then there were the gossipmongers. The people from college who just wanted to gawp. To be the first to update the SE14 Twitterverse, or get quoted in the papers as a 'friend of Dan's' when they'd never even spoken to him, not once, not ever.

I had been asked to read a poem at the service – to say something pretty and lasting – but in the end I bottled it. I stood up there with my eyes streaming, mute. Naomi walked up there to join me and took the paper from my fisted hand. She was crying then too, but she put her spare arm around me and read the lines out, two verses from a mediocre yet tragically poignant song Dan had written. It choked up the whole congregation, even the tweet whores.

I'd managed to pull myself together for the wake. The alcohol probably helped. Ditto the nicotine and the change of scene from church to pub. I couldn't touch the buffet – crisp triangles of egg sandwiches and burnt cocktail sausage rolls – but I did manage to rest both my elbows on the bar and sink a few quick shorts. I chatted and joked with other friends about the stupid things Dan had done. I threw up in the toilet and let out a few sneaky tears. I drank the vodka from my bag and reapplied my make up. When his band played I couldn't watch. They were shit without him. Halfway through the first ballsed up song I was huddled under a heater in the beer garden, chain smoking. People got pissed. A book was passed around to write memories of Dan in. I didn't put pen to paper, I didn't need to write us down to remember. I could still see it all – hyperreal. I could still feel him. Taste him on the roof of my mouth. I could still hear his quickened breath. I must have fallen into a taxi home for the next thing I remember is Maggie tucking me in like I was five again. Her stroking my hair while I drifted asleep.

After the funeral, at surface level, nothing really changed. My time drifted between college classes and the room of fog, all in a state of semi-consciousness, of deeply buried shock. Essays still got written and grades barely slid, but UCAS deadlines did not register. Where before I had held grand ideas of studying at St Martins, Goldsmiths or the Royal College then launching myself into the public consciousness, now the future seemed beyond thought or capability. For now the present was hard enough. The Days Without Dan.

*

It turned out that when Allan had said 'Not too early,' he had meant after brunch, lunch and perhaps even dinner, for his car did not reappear outside the hotel lobby until 7 p.m. In the time leading up to that I had called his cell repeatedly, such that reception had called me to check everything was okay. I had painted my nails, managed to dry all of my hair with the asthmatic dryer, and found an internet café from which I e-mailed my best mate. I'd been refused beer at the hotel bar because I was only nineteen, my adultness rebuked, and instead drank the last of my vodka – bought to cushion any delays at Heathrow – mixed with coke from the vending machine, from one of the tiny plastic glasses in my room; a guilty child. I'd stared at the absurd exhibits of humanity sunning themselves in the courtyard below before changing scene to the plush armchairs of the lobby, where there seemed to be lots of people who looked like they might be famous, but I didn't know who they were, and yet more people who really were famous but whom I'd missed because they slummed it so well. I had panicked – 'What if that was it?' I had cried crocodile tears, then reapplied my make-up and changed my outfit three times. I hadn't left the hotel for longer than the thirty-minute internet trip because my own mobile didn't work in the US. All in all I was pissed off and terminally bored when he breezed in. I had been sullen and silent, because if I spoke I couldn't tell whether it would make me yell or cry and I didn't want him to see that it mattered.

*

When I went to get my own passport last year, an adult one, I signed the wrong name on the form. I had to ask for a new one. The woman at the Post Office looked at me oddly – I think she sniffed out my Romany gypsy blood, my Irish tinker ways, but she didn't say anything. I signed the wrong name because it is his surname and not my mother's on my birth certificate. I use a known-as name the rest of the time, so that Mum and I have the same name. It makes life easier. At the time I worried that the Post Office woman had put a big black cross or a 'QUESTIONABLE' stamp on my form when I handed it all over, but if she did it hadn't stop me getting my burgundy booklet back through the post. Inside my photographed face looked slightly startled. It seemed strange placed in a portrait shot, rather than posing in my usual online identity's petulant chin-jutting profile. I had just turned eighteen. Mum had said that perhaps I should change my name, by deed poll, to officially be the same as the one I used. If that was what I would like to do – no longer have to use Allan's for official things, for anything. I wasn't sure what I wanted. Part of me hated my given surname, that piece of him lingering on in my life as well as hers long after he had buggered off and left us. Part of me still hoped he would turn out to be Superman. That he would come back and save me from the burning wreck of my life. That part concentrated on what ifs. If I changed my name, how would he ever find me? Stupid, but true.

*

My extremely tardy father drove me to Venice Beach as if he knew he'd done me wrong. I could tell he hated the place, and by night there was little of the desired people-watching to be done on the deserted promenade. Instead I took a photo of the full moon over the pier and managed half a smile at the mention of margaritas, of which I drank two, and felt the angered knots within me loosen like an after-hours office worker's tie.

I had asked easy questions about him and his job at the airport and filled in some of the gaps of his mundane day-to-day. Check-ins and staff shortages, shift cover and the ensuing endless-Starbucks-supply perk. Our talk was punctuated by the erratic ringtone of Allan's cell as a woman from Taiwan rang, and then another from Hong Kong. Both wanted to speak to me but I found it difficult to understand their aggressive broken English, they seemed to be fighting for a territory I had long given up claim to. As he showed me their photos, their smiles falling in poses held too long, Allan fell off the invisible pedestal I had helplessly been letting him occupy. He was just a sad old man clinging to his youth through freelance 'girlfriends', needing two to eclipse his forty-eight years. The thought – or my mounting blood alcohol level – made me feel sick. We called it a night, and I made it to my hotel room without drama. I spent the rest of the night dozing in and out of bad dreams with the TV for company. Thinking about Dan.

It had been Dan's idea that I should find Allan. He had made the search into his own little project. He was good with all that technical stuff; it was as if he'd been wired into the grid at birth, it all came so naturally to him. I got the gist of things that benefited me – how to access rare and new music, update my blog, and keep in touch with my mates – but beyond that it bored me. I liked my record player and mixtapes. I liked my books. Yet it was Dan who had found the family tree. There was some uncle that I'd never met who had traced my whole family's genealogy and published it online. It had only taken a couple of short brave e-mails from there, though it took me several months to send them. Dan and I'd had a stupid row and split up, although neither of us actually wanted to. We were both too stubborn to back down and then it had been too late.

It wasn't until after Dan's funeral that I sent the e-mails. He didn't live to hear me say 'okay' and see me type those lines on my keyboard, but I felt I owed it to him to try to do some of the things we had talked about. To live as many of the dreams we had dreamt as I could without him, all those plans that a drugged-up gloom had prevented him from completing. I wished he could have been around to hold my hand and pour my vodka. Somehow though, he'd felt close when I sent the e-mails, booked the ticket and packed my bags. As if he were sat on my bed, leaning into the corner of the room, his T-shirt riding up to show the line of dark hairs that stretched up from his waistband like an arrow, pointing to his sharp mind, his thoughtful face. His DMs discarded, his bare toes tapping out the rhythm of the music onto my leopard printed thigh. I had poured his apparition a drink too; clinked our glasses and drunk both.

*

Ring. Ring.

    Ring. Ring.

    I grabbed for the receiver and missed.

    Ring. Ring.

    'Hello?'

My voice croaked, dry.

    'Amy? It's Allan. I'm in the lobby, are you dressed?'

I looked down. Technically I was dressed, but not in anything I'd be seen dead in by anyone else. Half of last night's crumpled outfit and half of my pyjamas.

    'Erm, not quite, I'll be down in a minute... or, erm, five?'

*

I exited the lift looking every inch a starlet, not. More like the ghost of one. Giant shades eclipsed half my white face, and any grace I may have possessed had been replaced with a stronger than usual gravitational pull on my limbs that hunched my back and slowed my movement, creating a crooked, juddering walk. Jet lag.

    'Oh dear, somebody's hungover.'

    Allan had spotted me first. I didn't correct him.

    'You better get a couple of these down you before we head to Hollywood or you'll scare all the tourists.'

I did as I was told, wincing as the first cup scraped down my throat and rejoicing as the sugar and caffeine started to work its magic on the third.

*

The city was simmering, cooking its population slowly as Allan and I criss-crossed LA on the magical mystery tour of his absence from my life. Places he'd lived, worked, girlfriends he'd loved or escaped, the swanky places he'd drunk in before his business had gone bust, the office condo he'd slept in for eight years afterwards. He made no apologies – it was as if he were telling an old schoolfriend what he'd been up to since they parted. I listened intently and tried to work out what it was that had attracted my mother to him beyond the quirkily British good looks – a film noir Michael Caine – silver screen features he'd since lost. At home Maggie didn't talk about Allan much, and though curious, beyond my toddler 'Dadda?' stuck record, I'd never asked her; instead grasping at dislocated glimpses, a join-the-dot dad. Wistful words were delivered with a pained expression and lingered like a bad smell: 'He was the love of my life.' A decade and a half later and Allan certainly seemed charming and, as he told me anecdotes of his time in America, I discovered that we shared the same sense of humour – mostly dry, occasionally incredibly puerile. There were moments when I could even believe I liked him, yet they were fleeting.

We'd found a breeze to whip some colour back into my face by the Korean Friendship Bell. On the grass before it a magazine photographer shot hyperactive children while too many assistants got in the way. Allan caught the bug and pulled out a disposable camera. He took a photo of me squinting at the sun in front of the ornate bell. A man with thick glasses and skinny legs beneath his khaki shorts offered to take a picture of us. Afterwards, thanking the man, Allan had said:

'Ah, but who is she?'

'So long as your wife doesn't know, who cares?' Khaki Shorts replied, guffawing.

It was the worst sound I had ever heard, especially when Allan joined in. I thought of my mother and shrugged away from our still-clasped pose. Below cargo ships spilled their brightly coloured guts onto the docks.

On a good day, when Mum's evening crutch of wine was making her happily tipsy rather than morose, and when her latest affair was going to plan, she would conjure up the cocktail parties of her theatrical youth and I would sit and watch her perform for me. On those few occasions I would get caught up in her act, and for a few minutes I would believe that my father must have been a good man, a talented man, a man I'd want to know. At the end of her regaling, Maggie's face would fall in disappointment, she would 'come to' realising that life was no longer so, that life had only briefly been so dazzling. It was painful to watch, it was one of the reasons I hadn't told her of my plans to see Allan during my travels. I'd seen that hurt expression too many times. Those puppy-on-Prozac peepers.

Allan and I wandered the short distance to the Sea Lion Sanctuary where sick, bloated mammals lolled and wailed miserably on the slippery concrete beside the pool. Lonely Californian sea lions lay waiting, if not for freedom, then for feeding time. The place depressed me, so we had cut and run to the car. Allan drove us down a long winding descent, through landslide territory, to a small rocky beach, deserted but for a police car and a white pick-up truck. Beside the truck a man was being pulled up from his kneeling position on the floor – his arms in handcuffs – and shoved into the back of the cop car. As Allan parked his Ford, both of the other vehicles were snaking back up the dirt track. '*Hello*

America!' I thought. It was just like an episode of *CSI*.

On the flight on the way over, when I had tried to imagine LA I hadn't thought of beaches, or red sandstone cliffs, where land literally just broke away under foot, the earth crumbling and sliding away. I had instead thought of airbrushed people and million dollar smiles, of Hollywood, of *Pretty Woman* on Rodeo Drive, of growing up in *Beverly Hills, 90210* with neon lights and silicon dreams. My father's LA was practically suburban. He lived near and worked in the airport. He ate at Hong Kong Buffet and other budget all-you-can-eat for $8.99 places, and he gave them his all. When we reached the in-your-face wealth of Beverly Hills, Allan was shifting uncomfortably in his seat as much as I was. He parked up outside a house whose owner he claimed to be pals with. He made no move to drop in and I couldn't decide whether he was telling me the truth.

Walking away from the car I followed my father as he turned left and then right and suddenly there were stars beneath our feet. Framed within grubby pink slabs, many scarred with cracks. The golden points traced a social history from obscure actors to renowned jazz musicians before reaching a girl lying beatific on the ground beside 'David Bowie' while her mother straddled her and snapped one for the album. I rolled my eyes at Allan. Lining the streets in between brassy hotels were gift shops selling tacky tourist tat – their window displays boasting faded maps of Hollywood crime scenes jostling for space next to joke-shop sex paraphernalia.

Two scrawny, laddered Spidermen jumped in front of the same little girl and made her cry. One muttered something, bouncing a ball on a string of web, and the other turned on his heel and huffed off; a turf war of the not-so-looky-likes fleecing parents for pricy photo opportunities. Images that my own childhood albums were devoid of. I felt disappointed with the Walk of Fame in much the same 'Is that it?' way as I had been when I'd lost my virginity. At least sex had the potential for improvement. Hollywood had no such chance.

*

Natalie Wood must have been no taller than a doll, I decided, placing my giant size seven feet beside the imprints made by the film star's tiny heels. Tourists jostled all around me on the concrete autograph book that makes up The Chinese Theatre's famous forecourt. I sidled past the ample backsides of shrilling middle-aged females and their even larger husbands, to read the Marilyn Monroe quote on a sign by the wishing well. Then, upon snugly sliding my feet into Cary Grant's imprints; I became momentarily caught up in the glamour of a Hollywood past and found myself toying with the Blonde Bombshell's suggestion that 'anything is possible'. Had it been so for Maggie, my mother? I wondered what would have happened if she hadn't met Allan – I'd seen the newspaper clippings, I knew Mum was once really good, she could have been a film star. Without my father she might have succeeded, really made it. Without me in tow she could have caught a plane to Hollywood and plunged her hands and feet into wet concrete; made her mark as an applauded starlet. Despite Mum's photo albums – the scrapbook of plaudits and nostalgia back in my London home – I found it was hard to envisage such a scene now. Difficult to imagine her plunging into anything but a bottle or another adulterous relationship. She had a thing for unattainable men. If it was meant to be a form of self-protection – she wouldn't have to get too close, because it wasn't real – it never panned out that way. Mum bought season tickets for a rollercoaster ride, as far as her emotional life was concerned – one of the big dippers. Each man, whether married or just passing through town, became a sticking-plaster that was applied again and again to a scab that never healed; the wound inflicted by Allan leaving.

Sometimes my mother blamed me for her failed life, her shattered dreams:

'This is all your fault, you ungrateful child. Your father would never have left if I hadn't been pregnant with you. I should have aborted you then. I should have forced myself to miscarry. You broke all my dreams.'

Such spiteful words. I believed her as a little girl. Mummy was so upset, all the time, and Daddy had gone. Had mostly gone. They had relapses; it was messy. I thought it must be my fault. Maybe I wasn't pretty enough. Maybe I'd done something bad when I was really tiny, too tiny to remember. Later on Mum and I switched familial roles. She was the teenager shouting that she wished I'd never been born, but I would never dream of saying such things, no matter how angry I became. I was glad I'd been born. I knew that she was too, I'd heard her say it enough when she had thought I was sleeping. She'd pull the duvet over me, switch off the lamp and mumble on about how she didn't regret a thing. Often her voice would slur, and her breath would be hot with fermented grape, but it was her temper, not alcohol, that made her lie, that turned the volume up on her mean side.

Knowing that I was wanted at home caused the image of my runaway father to morph from the sometime-good-guy into the always-bad-guy, the gun-toting, heartless, cheating baddie. Mum was often so quiet, so unforthcoming with information about my father and their past. It was her friends who filled in some of the gaps. Their loud banter and stories would reach me in my eavesdropping spot on the landing well past my bedtime. At other times, they'd flock like flies in the kitchen, fixing drinks to take out onto our square of lawn. They painted his dark side for me, leaning forward to grab my chin in their pincers, leering:

'Such a pretty little thing.'

'Her father's eyes, without a doubt.'

'You think?'

She waved a sweet in front of my face: 'Sure. Look at how they wander after pieces of sugar.'

'Rose! Amy take no notice of her now, run along and play.'

By my teens I'd joined enough of the dots to convince myself I didn't need to know my dad. I tried to think of him as dead. Occasionally it would dawn on me that he could be, for all I knew. Good, I'd say. It is better that way. Still, the vision of him as the good guy would drift back in from time to time and I'd grab hold of it like a comfort blanket. As for Mum's harsh words – her sudden mood swings – I had learned to let them wash over me mutely while holding her wrists with a gentle force to stop her throwing things. It didn't work every time, but mostly I could try to stay statue still like that until the anger subsided and then hug her when, eventually, the shouting gave way to tears. 'Don't leave me, Amy,' she would plead with me then. 'Please, don't leave me alone here too. Promise me?' I let her down. There had been a time, many times, when I made that promise, and many more when I said nothing. She had let me leave her for this trip, she had to now that I was nineteen, but I could see that she remembered those promises. I recognised that look of betrayal in her eyes.

I looked up and saw my father standing awkwardly on the sidewalk, squinting against the late afternoon sunlight to try and find me among the crowd. I waved and walked over to him; spying his face filled with relief. He smiled at me and I didn't know what to do with it, I had assumed this trip was just delayed duty on his part, yet his expression when he spotted me suggested he was possessed of a deeper level of care for me than I could even begin to comprehend. A care that did not match his long, silent absence from my life. Sidestepping such thoughts, I said:

'Okay, I'm done. Tackville tourist box ticked. Let's get out of here.'

*

The smell of hot pizza filled the car as we pulled up in a suburban cul-de-sac in Gardena dotted with neat hedges and white houses. Crossing the unnervingly silent street, I followed Allan up a drainpipe-thin path beside a house whose garden was heady with tropical plants, fruit trees and bonsai shapes to a garage behind.

'Welcome!' he said, opening the side door with flourish. 'It's not much but it is mine.'

We walked past the fridge and the folding table bearing packaged goods – neon biscuit packets, tinned fruits and exotic juices – and up three small steps into the main space; a misnomer. The air was cold, a shock from the warmth of outside. A corrugated metal garage door took up the entirety of one wall. A rail of shirts and trousers lined the room like skirting board. Fake flowers sprouted from above curtain rails and behind the mirror, the touch of an unmentioned female. A double bed took up half the room: covered in plush boudoir throws, it seemed out of place – a high class whore's platform hidden in a hovel. In front of it two shabby chairs pointed towards the TV, under which lived a mountain of videotapes. A small cockroach scooted across the floor by my foot but I pretended not to notice, and instead kicked at the base of the dresser.

'It's nice...' I offered. Allan squirmed, and then took the pizza boxes from me before heading to the makeshift kitchen to dish them out.

'I make the best chips, do you want some?'

I didn't really feel that hungry, and yet I was aware of how much my visit had sucked for both of us, so far. To compensate I yelled back brightly,

'Sure do!'

My breath left frosty trails in the air. In an attempt to keep warm I circled the room and was surprised to see cute framed photos of my toddler self on the wall and dresser. One showed my short hair curling over one big blue eye, my crooked smile revealing rabbit-like teeth as I bit at the mince pie cradled in my gloved hands, the garden carpeted with thick snow. In another I pointed at fluffy creatures in the zoo with my hair tied in bunches and my head held to one side. I was dressed in denim dungarees and scuffed red Mary Janes. This unexpected trip down memory lane caused me to struggle to breathe. I was so taken aback that he still even had these pictures, let alone that they took pride of place in his home. I had had no contact with Allan for seventeen years. I coughed violently as all the illusions of my father's indifference crashed down. I fell into a seat by the TV, blinking back tears, wondering who had sent him these shots: a relative? A friend?

I don't know what I had expected to find. My ideas of my father were a jumbled mess. I'd held a constantly shifting picture of him in my head, changing from superhero to devil and back again. The images boomeranged but he didn't ever come home. He was an enigma to me, puzzling and mysterious. He had this film star quality because of it; especially because he'd left for America, for Los Angeles – City of Angels. To me he was the guy killed off in the first series of a TV drama, and the rest of the cast, after five minutes of hysterics and a glamorous funeral, carried on as normal and barely mention him. Like an *Eastenders* character who moved on from Albert Square but never visited again once they had

moved out of the vortex; just one tube stop away. In imagining
my father, even in those Superman rescue fantasies, I hadn't
placed myself amid his life in the aftermath. Before my flight
to LA, though, I had given some thought to how our first
conversation would go. If I am honest I had imagined a fight.
I had imagined weeping and whimpering. I hadn't ever
expected to find his life had played out like the storyline of
Slumdog Millionaire in reverse. Nor had I expected to find
that I brought anything but a flicker of guilt to his mind. I
had wanted to meet the man responsible for fifty per cent of
my genes; that was all. To see where I had come from, in order
to keep on moving.

*

Allan bumbled into the room bearing plates of pizza and chips.
I was still doubled up and so he called over,

'You okay over there?'

I mustered all my strength and got up, not looking at him
as I passed, muttering

'Fine, just got a hair caught… where's the bathroom?'

'Through the door, and on your right,'

I pulled the curtain-as-door shut behind me and sat on the
toilet trying to regain my composure. My mirrored self eyeballed
me. I breathed in long and deep, noticing the chip fryer cooling
in the corner by the bathtub as I did so. My dad's cobbled-
together abode was so different to what I had imagined, and so
like the darkened houses I had been trying to escape from; full
to bursting with the same air of disenchantment; just like my
mother's. It made me all the more determined not to be another
casualty of the mediocre, to live my life instead of letting it
slowly leave me bit by bit until I took up my grave. I drank some
water from the tap and went to rejoin Allan downstairs.

He was watching an old Bruce Lee film, and gestured at

me to join him, a plate of pizza congealing on the chair beside him. As I took my seat I heard the sound of police cars. Eventually I realised that it wasn't coming from the TV but instead from the road outside, their flashing lights casting the whole room as a disco. Allan and I looked at one other, both wondering what the other had done.

'LAPD! Open up!'

A fist hammered the door and Allan got to his feet, mumbling 'It's probably nothing.' As he walked towards the door I convinced myself that he looked guilty as sin and plotted both my alibi and my escape simultaneously. I'd watched enough American films, I knew the drill. I craned to hear the conversation beyond the closed door to no avail. After a while it swung open, revealing my dad in silhouette.

'They've come for you,' he joked.

I didn't move.

'Just kidding, kid, they want to have a little look around though and we have to stay put.'

'Why? What do they think they'll find? Are you in trouble? Are we in trouble?'

'No, nothing like that love.' Allan paused and looked hard at my face, trying to gauge whether to tell me the truth as if deciding whether a child was adult enough for a PG film. He sucked a breath in.

'The thing is, somebody shot a policeman just across the block and they think that the gunman is hiding in our street.'

When I realised he was no longer kidding I did not panic, I grinned. I couldn't help myself: now *this* was the America I'd expected.

Confused, Allan continued. 'They are going to search the house, which won't take long will it? Then we have to stay here until they give us the all clear, which could be a couple of hours or even a couple of days. I'm sure it'll all be sorted out soon though, it's a short street.'

'Wow! Sorry, but wow! This is really exciting!' Saucer eyes engulfed my face. I wasn't afraid; I knew that there was nowhere to hide in Allan's box of a home. 'Does this happen often?'

'No, but sometimes, this is LA.'

Two policemen blinded us with searchlights before getting to work with their manhunt, pulling the bed out and knocking clothes from the rail; their dogs finding nothing but bugs lurking.

'Okay, clear!' one barked from the bathroom.

'Yep, clear!' yelled another from our room. Then, to Allan, 'You sure you ain't seen nothing? It happened less than half a block away. You hiding something? Let me see your ID. Both of you.'

Allan pulls out his work ID and I fumble and find my passport in my bag.

'Alright, alright. Well he's not here, lock the door behind us when we leave and don't open any windows. You are not permitted to leave the house, for any reason, until we return to say you may. Understood?'

We nodded.

'Can I take a photograph of you?' I asked the officers.

They scowled. 'Ma'am this is not TV, we're not shooting a scene from *The Wire* or *The Shield*, okay? Now get outta my way, we've got important business to do.'

They marched out, oblivious to my pout.

Allan appeared unsettled. He followed the officers to the door and locked and bolted it behind them. He circled the garage, checking and double-checking the windows.

'Sit down, you're making me dizzy!' I exclaimed.

He hesitated then did as I'd asked. He seemed to be searching for something to say. After many false starts he spat it out.

'I'm sorry.'

I pretended I hadn't heard him. He said the words again.

'I'm sorry Amy, love.'

I narrowed my eyes and shifted in my chair. Something clicked in my mind, turning me waspish, mean. I couldn't stop myself from letting all those years of anger bubble to the surface. I threw a spear: 'Sorry for what exactly, Allan?'

As he visibly reeled back from this I silently tallied up his crimes, those almost forgotten upon finding such a humbled, fallen man. Breaking my mother's heart. Strike one. Abandoning his child, who wasn't even walking yet, with a woman who was almost certainly having a nervous breakdown. Strike two. Moving to the other side of the world and making no attempt to keep in contact. Strike Three. Out. So why was I here? I sighed.

'I'm sorry this trip has turned out so terribly, I'm not good with kids, I'm not used to being around them.' He rubbed his palm over his face, pulling at the downturned corners of his mouth.

'Well I'm not a kid any more; you missed out on that, huh, Dad!' My tantrumming words were poisonous, my face flashed with hate.

Allan looked older and greyer, pained, but he continued,

'I know. I'm sorry for that too. For not being around for you. But I can't undo it.'

Still baying for a fight, I instead finally gave in to tears and stopped shrugging off my father's attempt at a hug.

'I never stopped thinking about you, you know.'

'Sssh!' I hissed into his damp shirt angrily. 'Just stop. Enough now.'

After my sobbing had subsided we watched action movies in companionable silence, wrapped in blankets against the cool of the room. Each lost in our own thoughts.

*

At 1 a.m. Allan shook me awake.

'They got him, the gunman. He was next door, hiding in the hot tub with the lid on. A pretty close call, he wasn't far from us after all. Not one bit.'

He handed me a drink. I took a gulp before spraying the contents of my mouth everywhere in disgust.

'Ugh! What *is* that? It tastes like Germolene.'

My face screwed up like a pug dog.

'Root beer, well rum and root beer; I figured a drink was in order.'

'People drink that? Americans are weird.'

I wiped at my mouth while Allan located the Pepsi and refilled my glass.

'Thanks.'

'Are you packed? Do you still want to go tomorrow? I can change your flights.'

'Yes. No. Sort of. It won't take me long, I didn't even unpack properly.'

I thought for a minute.

'I think I should stick to the plan, for now at any rate.'

'San Francisco? You'd have more fun in New York.'

He meant there would be less hippies there. I saw how he'd slid towards conservatism with age. Hard, steady work and dormant Church of England teachings. He may not practise what he preached but he thought in terms of rules, at least for women. San Francisco was a must-see for me though. Clichéd as it was I wanted to trail The Beats in North Beach, read Ferlinghetti in City Lights and swap a poem for a beer in Versuvio. I needed to dance up Haight Ashbury to Amoeba Records to watch Devendra Banhart do an instore, and then sit a while in Golden Gate Park. I didn't say all this, I shrugged and replied: 'Then I'll go there too, later.'

'But what are you going to do? When you're there? With your life? What about uni?'

I ran my hands through my hair and bit my lip. It was hard to take, this man who had been AWOL for almost all my life, telling me where I would have more fun and demanding to know my career plans. Like he knew me. As if, in a couple of days, he could have gathered all the nuances of my character that he should have learned minute by minute, day by day, year by year from the beginning. I looked up at him: 'That is exactly what I'm on this trip to figure out, Dad. It could take a while but I expect that I'll be fine.'

Allan looked unconvinced yet unable to wield any parental power now, while I smiled, realising that it really was fine. I really was okay, or at least that was what I told myself.

*

My face burnt red as I waited for my dad on the shiny marble forecourt of the hotel, avoiding the amused looks of the valet boys who had helped Allan open his car the other night. I felt dirty in my jeans and crumpled tee, my round-the-world backpack resting at my feet, as bellboys wheeled out brassy rails of classier wardrobes. The panic started to rise: for the rest of my journey I was on my own. For eight months or twelve or more. The time of my next flight was fast approaching. The anxiety built and bang, my nerves shot. Where was he?

Right on cue Allan's silver Ford appeared. He got out, jangling his keys in the direction of the watching valet boys who mock-cheered.

'Ready?'

I nodded and Allan threw my bag into the backseat.

'We're cutting it fine but if worst comes to worst I can check you in. I have to park up and get the shuttle bus over so I'll drop you off and you can try the queue. Standby looks pretty clear this morning so you should be fine.'

*

I hiked my rucksack onto my bare shoulders as Allan drove off. Entering the air-conditioned expanse of flight departures I located the desk I needed and headed over. My face fell as I saw the convoluted line of disgruntled passengers, all waiting, and all now cutting it fine. A Latino woman with short-person complex came over and bossed passengers around. She snapped orders and then, as an aside, sniped: 'If you're due to fly in the next hour you aren't going to make it.'

People groaned, and the queue became a confusion of trolleys and families uncertain what to do next. I felt sweat forming on my back, and tried to keep calm as I watched the minutes tick round and round the face of the giant white clock on the wall ahead. I had moved forward mere inches when I spied Allan rush through a staff door in his uniform and, after having a quiet word with a colleague, move to an available desk.

'Excuse me, sorry, excuse me!' I dodged people and ducked barriers and evil looks as I made my way to Allan's desk.

'You made it!'

'Only just. Right, how many bags are you checking in?'

I passed my one backpack over, revelling in the double novelty of my dad (a) doing something fatherly and (b) checking me in.

Once I had my boarding pass, and Allan his own for his impromptu trip to visit Girlfriend Two in Hong Kong, we raced the clock to our gates. Belting up stairs only to be met with more queues; we instead opted for a cheat route. Scrambling across the shined floor of the terminal, Allan flashed his staff pass to rush us past regular passengers and through hurried bag and shoe checks until we reached his turning for international flights.

'It's been good to meet you,' he said warmly.

'Yes, you too!' I took a snapshot with my eyes. Click. Part of me thought it could be the last. Even as he said:

'Stay in touch, e-mail me.'

He hugged me tightly, quickly, before releasing his grip.

'Now, run!'

I kissed him on the cheek and legged it to my gate, arriving breathless at the desk.

'I'm flying standby. Have you called the names?' I wheezed at the attendant.

'Yes, yes I have, but you're on the flight, you can board now.'

I thanked him and took my seat in first class just as the gate closed. As the stewardess began to mime pulling down oxygen masks and the nearest emergency exits I sank back into the chair, more exhilarated than exhausted. I closed my eyes and pictures of Dan danced on the inside of my eyelids. I opened them again. Through the porthole window the ground fell away from me, leaving a Hollywood blue screen of a sky in its place – a starting point upon which anything could be pasted. Arrivals and Departures where, if anybody was waiting for me, they didn't know it yet.

Maggie

The crack was getting bigger. Maggie was certain of it. As the
two teenage girls next door wailed familiar eighties power
ballads on their new karaoke machine, the gash-like scars
shook, elongating with each high note. Cut deep into the
peachy walls they spawned hairline fractures; like those in
her dishwasher-unfriendly wine glass.

The jagged unstitched tracks erupted out of the top right
corner – just above the cobwebs – and coursed down the walls,
choking the clock as it tick-tocked through the midnight minutes;
tearing the room's skin wider open with each slamming door.
Maggie lay motionless in the yellowed strip of artificial light from
the SE14 street, continuing to wait out the fight, the night. Boots
thudded down stairs before a front door clicked open and
banged shut. Sighing in resignation Maggie realised that it was
no good. Even before World War III kicked off at number 12,
she had known sleep would not be forthcoming. Sleep had long
stopped being her friend and playmate, and the night's earlier
events were certainly not helping.

She kicked back the quilted layers of stars and pastel
patches, before flicking on the dim bedside lamp. Shivering,
she pulled a discarded cardigan over her curved shoulders to

combat the winter chill that assaulted her duvet-warm skin. Tired eyes re-adjusted to the newly light room. The angular red numbers of the digital alarm clocked in at 00:37, and two hours after going to bed here she was, still wide awake, her dreamland as evasive as ever. Was the house too quiet, the street too loud, or the bed too empty? The answer was all three, and more, yet this knowledge would not bring Maggie her much needed rest; *au contraire*. Years of parental programming for a socialite teen meant that, even though her daughter had absconded from South London a fortnight prior in search of global adventure, part of Maggie's brain still lay in wait for the jangle of her keys, the scratching at the lock, the stumble and muffled laughter on the stairs that let her know she was home and safe. Now cast aside, the forgotten mother lay in wait only for morning, the nest a yawning emptiness.

Maggie read and reread the same line of a novel five, maybe ten, times and still could not take it in. Lately her concentration was not up to much, replaced with the fuzzy brain distraction of TV and alcohol. Yet to join ranks with the cable revolution, and with a daughter who was more into music and books than three hundred TV channels, the clunky old box in the corner of the room only had five options, three of which appeared to be devoted to reality TV by day, and phone-in quiz shows at the hours Maggie's sleeplessness had her crawling the walls. She watched these marathon TV shows, drained, for the noise, the company. In truth she was hooked on the soap opera drama, the high gambling stakes.

Images of her ruined evening clogged her mind. Maggie certainly needed some distraction now, anything to keep from dwelling upon it. She almost craved the rising panic that only liberal parents could get; the anxiety that consumed her in the hours after she'd allowed Amy to go off to another stranger's party with no curfew and her blessing; hoping giving such freedom would be enough to ensure her daughter's safe return home. Were Amy simply out, and not away travelling, Maggie might fill these hours of her sleeplessness with neurotic worrying. She might be in bed, but awake, awaiting the teenager's homecoming. She could watch 2 a.m. come and go, with a bruised heart choking her, blocking the air's path from throat to lungs. She might fret that there'd been some bomb or other on the bus or the tube, or a gang knifing, and Amy had been injured. She could indulge in her wildest thoughts, allowing them to roam her mind; while every siren wailing past her window would suggest ever more possibilities. Then Maggie's demons would come out of the bedroom's shadows to taunt her.

She could, for just one second, wish Amy's father were still around to share the fear of these moments. Deep down, she knew that she was being irrational and that her teenager was probably safe. That she was just punishing her for the row that morning, or testing the strength of the boundaries that had been laid down. Or more likely than that, Amy just hadn't thought about it at all, distracted as teens are by the thrills and spills of adolescence. Of being a teenager. Of boys or girls or boys and girls. Of cider or spliffs, of looking old enough to go to the bar. Then Maggie's overactive imagination might be off again, entangled in all these new dangers, all her own mistakes at that age.

The clock would turn from 02:36 to 02:37 and Maggie might already be imagining smelling the pain and suffering of the clinical corridors of A&E. She might ring the hospitals, breathing a sigh of relief with each 'not admitted here' she heard. She would be getting up and peering through the net curtains to the street, looking for taxi headlights or the familiar sight of Amy and a mate swaying towards the house, unsteady on their feet. With no sign of her, Maggie might then be found breaking unwritten rules and ringing her daughter's mobile, only to find that the battery was dead, again. She would try to sound calm as she left her plea for a call back.

Maggie's anguish might really crank up and she would find herself trying to decide how much worse things would be if she started calling Amy's friend's parents. She would reach to the back of her underwear drawer and find the emergency cigarette pack and light up while she stalled herself. Her shaking hand might turn on Sky News 24, expecting to hear the news of her worst nightmares. She would ready herself, prepared to laugh at her own silliness, and as she did so the key would turn in the lock and Amy *would* be home to confirm it, giggly and unscathed. But not tonight, her daughter would not be walking back through her front door for another eight to twelve months. An eternity.

Maggie shook her head at her own neurotic inventions and lit a cigarette. Somehow, despite the fact that innumerable horrors really could be occurring to her daughter on her global travels, Maggie had the feeling that Amy was safe. She also knew that, were Amy home tonight, there was bound to be a mother–daughter row, a big blazing argument into which Maggie would throw all the hurt Simon had caused her. She would smash things up where earlier that evening she had stood in mute disbelief thinking 'Not again, not again, not again.' Instead, alone, she stumbled down the cold, creaking stairs in half-darkness. In the kitchen she grabbed the already-open bottle of supermarket Merlot from the kitchen table; ignoring the evening's burnt, abandoned dinner and the cat's mocking stare.

*

'Maggie, Magpie, I said a chat, not dinner...' he'd said. Then other things like:

'No, no there really isn't anything left to say...'

'Well if you'd prefer to think of me that way, that's okay...'

'You can't really have thought this was going somewhere?'

And then, softly, firmly: 'I have to go...'

He hadn't slammed the door. He had left his key. Maggie hadn't wanted to cry, but of course, she did.

They say that men like Simon never leave their wives.

*

Maggie's TV was on in the corner of her bedroom. A smarmy, permatanned host beamed his perfect smile at the camera.

'Complete this phrase. As sick as a...

Parrot

Puffin

Partridge

Penguin'

The question flashed on the screen below him.

'Caller number two, what's your answer?' His botoxed face showed no expression beyond the forced grin.

'Nooooo love, partridge is incorrect. Bad luck.'

The line went dead. The presenter began speaking – motormouthed – as if he were on speed, to excite his drunken audience at home into picking up the phone.

'I'm going to make things a little bit more interesting. I really want to give some more money away. Let's see if my boss will let us have a quickfire round.' He tapped at an earpiece and looked to his left.

Maggie couldn't help it; she was on the edge of her seat. She had become addicted to the rush of these shows as both observer and participant – she filled with excitement at the chance of winning big money, of watching somebody's whole life changing in one couch potato instance. It had become one of the highlights of her day, especially since Simon had dumped her and Amy had left on a jet plane. It was like the *Good Housekeeping* of gambling – talk of your winnings would be acceptable in polite conversation at the corner shop or the bakers. There was no way you could lose your house or your kid's inheritance. TV phone-in quiz marathons held none of the pathos or the cheap grimy boredom of the roulette wheels inside a high street casino; simply a world of opportunity at the end of your premium rate phoneline.

'He will. Fantastic! Get dialling there at home, you could be winning some serious cash prizes tonight. Caller number three, are you there?'

Maggie picked up the phone and dialled. A hyperactive automated voice answered.

'Congratulations, caller, you're in the queue and on your way to winning a serious amount of money. Hold on tight, we'll be right with you.'

A pop song blared down the line, interspersed with cheerleading phrases from the automated voice telling her that she was 'so, so close'. And that this could be her 'lucky day'. After five minutes Maggie hung up.

*

Since the spoiled dinner and the subsequent gloom it filled Maggie and her home with, her colleagues at the office had stopped expecting her to come in. She hadn't shut down completely: she could turn around the week's workload in just a few hours, and from home, so as long as she checked in for her post they tended to leave her alone. Maggie had been working there since Amy was old enough to go to school. She had toyed with the idea of going back to the stage, but she had been too afraid of failure, and the schedule would have been so impractical – the late nights of rehearsals and promotions, the socialising necessary for the cast to bond and let off steam. As a single parent it just wouldn't have been possible; she didn't want her little girl growing up all alone, being looked after by strangers instead of her own flesh and blood. She missed her old life, but she loved her daughter. As such she had needed a day job. Allan hadn't bought Amy anything more than an ice cream since she was born, and he'd sent neither a correspondence address nor any contributions towards his daughter's upbringing from his new home.

Maggie would buy the newspapers on the way back from dropping Amy at her primary school. She'd open them at the jobs pages, spreading the black and white sheets across the kitchen table, but then find herself absently staring into space. Occasionally she would circle an advert in red ink, one bloodshot eye staring back at her, but she never quite got around to filling out the application forms when they came. All those gaping spaces to fill with the details of her academic failures and career nose-dive. She couldn't bring herself to do it.

The hours that Amy was at school were instead spent with all the necessary chores a small child brings – doing laundry, fixing ripped clothes, cleaning, and food shopping. There would be about an hour of staring into space while her mug of coffee went cold. There was the time spent organising the pile of bills into two piles – 'pay or be cut off' and 'ignore'. Then, more pleasantly, there were visits from friends – a couple who were also mothers, and others from the stage who seemed impossibly glamorous among Maggie's makeshift and make-do home. It was one of the latter who mentioned the job to her after she refused to go back to acting.

The job was for an agent, and involved making coffee and organising a chaos of loose papers and files. It was neither flashy nor fascinating but it was within Maggie's capabilities and the hours suited Amy's school schedule. Besides, she had done far worse when she was saving up to move to London, any odd job for her parents' friends including some nasty cleaning sessions – Mr Davies's bathroom still gave her nightmares – and a job at the local chip shop where she'd return home every day reeking of chip fat and pickled eggs. Each time she wrapped up a greasy portion of cod and chips in a sheet or four of newspaper and saw one of her idols' faces staring back – Julie Walters, Sigourney Weaver or Meryl Streep – it reminded her of why she was there and where she was going. She would give her customers, who were the closest thing she had to an audience at the time, her best performance – showering them with dazzling smiles and acting as if she loved her job more than anything. So thrilled was she with her plans to reach a city spilling over with stages and good scripts far beyond the school talent shows or the am dram productions and pantomimes she had dabbled in thus far.

These days her employer's agency had expanded beyond recognition. There were new departments and bigger premises. The organisation now covered musicians, comedians, writers and the stars of stage and screen. Maggie had only recognised a fraction of the faces passing through her floor. When the time came to get out without losing her salary, a gentle mention of the word 'stress' to her line manager led them to a simpler 'flexible-working' solution. Maggie now managed to avoid the small talk and water-cooler gossip, carrying a reduced administrative role from home via e-mail and snail mail. Other than that she didn't really speak to anyone, except for the cat – Carbon, for he is *that* black – and the people on the end of quiz show phone lines. She used to leave messages after the beep on Simon's mobile – charming, confident... and then pleading, begging. He did not return her calls. He did get a new number.

*

The door to Maggie's bedroom flew open with a draught. The room flickered in the electrical blue light cast from the TV. The box's sound was turned off. A variegated trail of dresses, skirts, jumpers and undergarments clean and dirty had been strewn and trampled across the floor, chair, bed – every available surface. Lying among them were empty bottles, festering coffee mugs, used glasses, and Maggie. She was in bed with the quilt pulled over her head, tossing and turning – another day, another sleepless night. Amy was on her mind. She wriggled and huffed and then found herself getting up and walking downstairs to the computer. As the clunky old system fired up, she poured and gulped down a glass of Merlot. Then she started up Firefox. Amy's face looked back at her – a familiar and ridiculously sullen pose, her large inky eyes downcast, her father's lips painted red and pouting. Amy's polka-dot travel blog. Her daughter had set it as their internet homepage so that Maggie could keep in touch easily, so that she wouldn't lose the URL and complain about the lack of phonecalls: 'I'm going on a budget trip Mum. B-U-D-G-E-T. I can't be calling you every day, but I'll be writing updates here, like a diary, and putting photos here, and you see this... this is the map of my journey so you can track where I'll be and when.' Amy had written it all down for her and pasted the instructions to the wall by the machine 'just in case'.

Maggie wasn't completely useless when it came to PCs but for work she only used them for word processing, accounts and e-mails. She tended to call people to ask questions rather than look up the information on their website. She still found it quicker, and the human voices reassured her. She smiled as she read Amy's update on San Francisco – she had seen a lot, and so far she absolutely adored the Museum of Modern Art, all the second-hand bookstores and thrift shops. Lunching on burritos from Mission; drinking coffee and writing her journal in Café Trieste. Maggie flicked through the accompanying photographs – vibrant hilly streets ascended against cobalt skies, graffiti sprawled across Alcatraz, the Green Tortoise Hostel where she was staying – travellers gathered eating and chatting within the shabby ballroom, whose ornate ceiling hinted at former grandeur. There were more – Amy smiling in front of the Golden Gate Bridge, Amy with two boys on a boat trip, Amy reading in City Lights and Amy strolling into the sunset at Ocean Beach. Her daughter looked happier than Maggie had seen her in a long time, lighter somehow, and free.

There was another, smaller album – 'LA'. Maggie rubbed her head in confusion; she was sure Amy had said she was heading straight to San Francisco. She had wanted to go for years and years. She'd been so excited, pouring over her *Hippie* coffee table book and playing all her Arthur Lee, Janis Joplin, and Grateful Dead vinyl at top volume. The sad poignancy of her favourite Jefferson Airplane track – 'Don't you want somebody to love?' – swirling through the house. Maggie hadn't ever considered that Amy would lie; she'd never needed to before. The date of the LA album showed that it had only just been uploaded. She flicked through the pictures – the Hollywood sign, the Chinese Theatre, Natalie Wood's footprints – and then she backtracked suddenly. Maggie stared at one photo for a long time – Amy stood beside a much older man, his arm clasped around her shoulder, in front of a pagoda-like structure. The man was instantly familiar despite how the years had changed him. Tears dripped down Maggie's face. The photo caption read: 'I'm sorry, Mum. I didn't know how to tell you. I'll write properly soon.' Hours passed, no such e-mail came, but the bottle emptied.

*

The birds began their relentless chorus and vehicles chugged to life in the street outside the kitchen window. Next door's white van backfired as it juddered away. Maggie was seated at the rustic table, another empty bottle of wine and several loose photographs spread in front of her. The remnants of last night's dinner merely pushed to one side. Radio 4 had hushed conversations behind her back while she rested her head in her hands, her grey matter a blanket of dropped stitches – muddling, knotting, unravelling.

The lack of sleep and plenitude of alcohol was causing her mind to play tricks on her. Maggie imagined a younger Amy in the room with her, inflicting the silent treatment in that way she had at fifteen. Fidgeting close by. Sighing. Flicking her long, dyed hair. Getting the carton of orange juice out of the bottom of the fridge and standing before the open door slurping it really loudly. A silhouette of insolence. She never tired of it. Maggie had opened her mouth to speak, but as she did so Amy's apparition had clicked her tongue against her teeth and exhaled, rolling her eyes at her mother before throwing her bag onto one shoulder and heading out the door.

Maggie thought of her daughter before the trip, in those weeks after Dan's death, when she had seemed beyond reach. Visible, constantly around; and yet moving through the house as if within a bubble. She would career through the kitchen and open the door before her trail of sullen friends had even had time to rap their bored, bejewelled knock on the glass. Intercepting Maggie's smile, Amy would grab her mates by the hand and pull them through the doorframe, flashing her mother a 'What?' glare as she hormonally huffed past. Her usually immaculately kohled eyes were pink, the black make-up smudged, squashed spider legs sprawling down her ageing adolescent cheeks. Her face veiled in the ash-grey of sudden bereavement.

The funeral brought little relief. The forced cheer and splashes of colour. Amy's gaunt appearance and failed speech. Her later outburst at the pub, knocking the microphone stand over and yelling at Dan's mother:

'He did it to himself, for fuck's sake. He wanted to go. He left us all on purpose. Why are we fucking celebrating? Because he succeeded? Well he did, didn't he? He succeeded in getting out of his head and out of this world. The selfish bastard.'

Maggie knew that Amy wouldn't remember being put into the taxi, or being carried up the stairs at the other end. She wouldn't realise how Maggie had sat and watched over her until her breathing returned to normal, stroking the teenager's hair and pleading with God, the spirit, whoever it was that was in charge of these things to let her little girl have a better happier life than she had. For this funeral not to mark the start of the hurt, the pain.

The crying and stropping subsided after the funeral, yet the quiet that followed in its wake was even worse. Amy had appeared to be shut off from Maggie; she couldn't reach in and help her. She couldn't hold her daughter and say she understood, that she knew what pain was, she knew how Amy felt. Maggie felt her own malady throb and course through her veins as if Allan had left only yesterday. Seeing the bastard's face after all these years, sunny and assured next to Amy, brought it all back – the venom, the hate, and the love. She felt the former betrayal and abandonment again tenfold. Like father, like daughter. She didn't appraise him critically. She didn't notice how age had changed him for the worse. She looked at that photo and saw his face, all those years before, angered and spiteful, and it triggered all the old reactions stored and magnified over the years. Their combined actions left nobody but Maggie in that house – alone, neglected, and about to run out on herself as well. Still drunk, Maggie buttoned up her coat and shoved the A4 printout of Amy and Allan's holiday photo in among the junk of her handbag – the scrunched-up sweet wrappers, leaky biros, house keys, purse, lipstick, and yesterday's unopened mail. She bolted from the house, destination unknown.

*

On the Jubilee Line on the way to London Bridge the tube shuddered to a halt between stations. Maggie dreaded moments like this, when the lights flickered and dimmed and the air shrank. She feared them, not because she thought a terrorist attack – another 7/7 – was imminent; it was more that she couldn't stand the staying still, hanging. Each time it felt like she was being buried alive. Her sister Ella said there's a term for this, they use it at those awful call centres she trained at sometimes. White space. Not being anywhere. The tube jolted back into motion and Maggie dropped her shoulders and unclenched her fists. She returned her half-hearted attention to the nonsense news of the free paper on her lap, a plan of sorts forming in her head. She was not going to work; she couldn't face telling them about another failed relationship; she didn't want pity. She wanted chips and salted air. She was going to the seaside.

*

'You stupid cow!'

Maggie could hear the words, angrily spat in her direction, but couldn't see their source. Couldn't see his reddening face, the broken lens of his glasses, the gaping seam, splitting up the back of his too-tight pinstripe jacket.

'Why don't you look where you're fucking going, eh?'

She felt a kick, booted deep into her side, sending her coughing and spluttering back into consciousness. She was splayed out on a cold, grey platform, her skirt revealing more leg than most would think proper for a woman that age, half conscious, and bleeding. At 10.35 a.m. on an unordinary Friday on the concourse of Brighton train station.

Maggie tried to focus on the voice, hesitant, male, and floating down the aural tunnel towards her. Vision flashed back and then took its leave again, like a camera taking a photograph. On. Off. For a fraction of a second a circle of faces floated above her and beyond them a glass roof. She blinked. Twice. Her vision returned slowly, taking in the cracked, cheerless concrete; and her left arm sprawled as if it had been thrown and broken ahead of her. Somebody's shadow bent over Maggie, a fat-fingered hand helped her to sit upright, their palm clammy, their face obscured by saucer eyes. A squeaky Brummie accent spoke.

'Are you alright? You practically flew.'

He placed a bulging handbag down by her side. Maggie rubbed at her eyes and glanced behind her; the open train door was a good ten feet away. Blood was seeping through her woollen tights, torn at the knee, and her chin hurt like hell. She stared blankly at the young businessman's concerned face, dazed. The crowd was dispersing, the platform emptying.

'Can you remember what happened?'

She remembered standing to get off the train, a sudden boozy dizziness overtaking her, a giddying vertigo, even though both feet were firmly upon the ground. The crackle of the Tannoy faded as her consciousness just seemed to slip away. She grasped at it, her hand instead clutching at thin air and then the top of a chair, her body pulled sharply back down again, knocking the empty miniatures off the table. It was merely seconds before the pins and needles were easing as quickly as they had arrived. The blur of vision shifting from black to white space, edges returning, shapes shifting back into

3D. That end of the carriage had been virtually empty as other travellers' drunks radar had caused them to make a wide berth of Maggie. She had taken a deep breath and swept her hand over her frizzy hair. Chastising herself for being a silly cow, she had pulled her handbag over her right shoulder, and buttoned her coat. The train had stopped, and she had made her way out of the carriage. The automatic doors opened, and then she was plunged into sudden blackness again. Soaring off the edge of the world into nothingness; nowhere.

Somewhere, under the rainbow of voices, Maggie had tried to stand up, but her vision began to fade again and she lost her balance. It forced her to remain seated on the ground. Two green figures were walking purposefully towards her, station staff. Their uniforms commanded information and they had soon worked out the situation from the few stragglers still intrigued by the incident, the bit of commotion.

'She fell...'

'No, fainted, and practically flew out of the door.'

'No, fell, she was drunk as a skunk... all over the place.'

Their words jumbled until a softer voice bent in closer to Maggie, seeming to speak right inside her head:

'Hi there, I'm Mark, the station manager. You appear to have had a fall. What's your name?'

'Maggie.' Her mouth was parched. Her voice sounded far away, dry and brittle like breaking kindling. She felt like crying – as a child would upon falling – but instead she started to laugh, a few startled shrieks that bubbled into uncontrollable waves of giggles. Shock, they said. An ambulance was called. Water was fetched. She sat on that platform laughing like a lunatic for a full ten minutes. Time appeared to stop, to stretch and then snap. There was nothing but cascading snorting and chortling and a sensation of warm, wet tears washing down her worn cheeks.

A woman and child hurried past her, the child running ahead, bouncing, pointing, and accusatory: 'Why is that woman laughing, Mummy...? Mum!?'

'Ssshh! Haven't I told you that it's rude to point?' the woman had replied, looking straight through Maggie's sorry, sloshed state. The child had stared goggle-eyed at the laughing heap, before bounding towards the train and onto the next curiosity.

*

Patched up and refusing a trip to hospital 'just in case' – how she hated them – Maggie had hobbled past the pretty Lanes boutiques, stopping only to buy a new pair of tights and change into them before reaching the seafront. She was happy to be able to smell the strong salt-scent of the sea once again, to hear the screeching banter of the fat gulls circling overhead or nosediving for dropped chips on the rocky shore below. She felt at home with the winter sun, fiercely bright against the paper white sky, casting the wet pebbled beach and incoming tide a shimmering gold.

Young couples – wrapped up in scarves and each other – strolled along the Esplanade past the shuttered bars towards the dilapidated West Pier. Stripped of her former finery, the listed old lady appeared to be diving into the waters, escaping the pitiful gaze of passers-by. Maggie remembered dancing down the beach below her in the early 1980s, consumed with the first flushes of love, Allan chasing, his dark curls falling over his film-star face, his shirt flapping comically in the breeze. Breathless kisses. That was when she had liked him best, all to herself away from the showy distractions of their scene – the girls, the drugs, the never-ending parties. All those things that, coupled with tiredness and a stressful theatre role, could cause her to snap, forcing her cycle of mood swings to speed up and sound off more and more and more. In Brighton with Allan, all those fears, those insecurities, had faded away, and anything seemed possible. Maggie had gazed up at the concert hall and imagined performing to the bold and the beautiful Victorians, or partying with flapper girls in the 1920s, in long gloves, elegantly waving a fine black cigarette holder about the place. When she'd first arrived in London Maggie had been performing in the city's damp, tiny fringe theatres hoping for a kind critic, a big break. By the time she had met Allan the hoping had paid off. She was overjoyed, she was wild. Amidst all the excitement she fell hopelessly in love.

Maggie shivered, pulling her coat tighter against the chilling breeze, and wandered down onto the beach. As she picked her way across the pebbled shore Maggie had the feeling that she could walk forever – left, right, left, right – the movement became mechanical and numbing, while the wind whipped thoughts from her head. Up ahead a father scooped up a toddler running too close to the water's edge.

When Amy was a little girl she loved coming to the seaside. She wasn't afraid of the water at all. She'd race over the stones and up to the waves and point and giggle. When they were back in Wales, visiting Amy's Nanna in Swansea, she'd build intricate shell-covered castles with moats. Before her Bampa died – a heart attack – he would drive them down to Langland. There he would lead Amy over rocks, a small fishing net in his hand, and stoop over the rock pools patiently explaining all the things that Amy pointed and gasped at – seaweed and anemones and mussels and barnacles. The sand spirals caused by lugworms as seen at low tide. He had done the same with Maggie long before. His calloused hands placing treasures from the sea in her hands: 'There you go mermaid,' he would say as he passed over tideline trinkets, or slipped prewritten messages into washed up bottles.

'It's for you? That's magic that is love. Magic.' His eyes would twinkle and his wife would shake her head at him but smile and go along with it. He hadn't liked Allan from the start. He'd told her as much:

'I respect your decision love, I only want to see you happy is all.'

'Oh but I am, Tad, I am.'

*

Maggie had first met Allan at a closing night party mere months after moving to London from Swansea. Her hair was big, like the puffball skirt of her dress, and she was sparkling. She was having a wild old time – acting, modelling, partying, and drinking heavily. Happy with a rush of male attention and committed only to her hair dye and the stage. At first Allan hadn't spoken to Maggie, but he had glanced up and caught her eye for one 'don't breathe' moment. That was all it took. Hooked, yet he had taken his time reeling her in.

She had been getting some decent roles, and then finally she'd gained her break, a big part in a West End production. It was a dark and serious play and Maggie's hugely expressive eyes had won her the role. She'd held her audience transfixed and the city was abuzz with her name, The Next Big Thing. It was then that Allan had swooped in to charm her pants off. He'd wanted to be the man with the best new actress in town on his arm, his own trophy star.

In the beginning all was beautiful, a pairing that rang out with laughter, screamed with pleasure and reeked of true, new love. Theirs was a relationship that burned fast and bright, the room glowing when they collided, scattering splinters of coloured light as the crowd oohed and ahed, a human firework display. Later the explosions were less pretty and more noisy, until the day when Maggie had been left spinning alone, a petered-out Catherine wheel rebuked for other bright young things; an endless supply of disposable sparklers.

Maggie soon became so taken with Allan she hated to leave his side, and the endless parties and socialising began to take their toll. The hangovers were worse and seemed to drag on all day through work and until the next party, while Allan seemed unaffected, or maybe just never allowed himself to sober up. He floated on the word of her success and spent her hard-earned money. Occasionally he appeared as a bit part on TV or in a new film, one that favoured looks over talent and effort. She slogged away at her serious stage roles and he breezed through his screen time. Maggie's schedule became more and more demanding and she struggled to make daily rehearsals. The joy of performance drained from her with each show, for every night was another that she was not with her love. She saw her work as the thing keeping her away from Allan, and began to despise it.

Her acting started to suffer, as did her appearance, her skin taking on the sickly pallor of one who did not see daylight, and who rarely spent time outdoors. Tall tales were spreading through their own social circles and beyond, via the press, to the public. Photos of Allan with other prettier, younger women continued to turn up in the newspapers and magazines. Jealousy raced through Maggie's system like a drug. It was immense, and their fights, whether public or private, were outrageous, and yet while Allan's attention had more than wavered, his grip had not.

*

Maggie jumped as something crunched under foot, sending pain shooting up her bruised leg, wrenching her back to the present, the here and now. To her left an elderly couple sat in their own stripy deckchairs eating homemade triangular sandwiches, both quietly staring at the point where the sea met the sky as if they knew something that she didn't. Maggie turned and joined them in their watch for a while but saw nothing of consequence, and the riddles of her life remained unsolved.

*

On the advice of her agent Maggie took the '88 summer break to rest and unwind, enticing Allan to visit her parents and then hole up at a remote cottage in Gower for a couple of weeks that, despite the dismal weather, were still filled with sex and laughter. It couldn't last. The bright lights were fast calling Allan back; he'd desperately needed to be part of the action with people milling around gasping about how fabulous he and his girl were. He itched for it. He'd wanted Maggie to be the unusual free-spirited beauty he'd first fallen for, but she could only manage to act that free and easy, to ignore Allan's other girls, by drinking more, and then more again. She'd lost the confidence and vigour she'd had when she first came to London eager for a top billing, a slice of fame. She wasn't living up to her glittering promise – she knew it, and theatreland (both backstage and front of house) knew it – but Maggie was too distracted by her own life to perform as another character, to do another storyline any justice.

The gossip blazed across town and so did Maggie and Allan's relationship. The golden couple was fast losing lustre, and arguments tumbled like dominoes, one after the other, each one worse than the time before. They were a vicious pairing at war. Allan always wanted to win, to have the last word, and Maggie would needle and whine, blackmail and manipulate. She would throw things, she would drink excessively, and she would slap Allan hard across the face. Afterwards, their house would be carpeted in broken shards of glass or ceramic, partition walls would gape with holes where Allan had pounded out his anger – bang, bang, bang. After hysterically pleading with him not to go, not to leave her, Maggie would inevitably find herself left alone, sitting among the debris of their fights while Allan drank his way across town and into somebody else's knickers. He would return home to find Maggie passed out on the sofa. The mornings after the row before were all sweetness and light, on Maggie's part. She'd act as if nothing untoward had happened – no awful words were spoken, no tears shed. They both would. Allan would emerge to a tidied flat, a big smile and a cooked breakfast. He could read the newspaper uninterrupted while Maggie readied herself for work and left quietly.

When the rows became all that existed within the relationship, he ditched her. He left Maggie, fragile, weeping, and, unbeknown to her, pregnant. He absconded from fatherly responsibilities and all the other trappings of parenthood and marriage; the boredom of settling down in one place and with one woman. He was restless and by the time Amy was learning to talk, Allan had fled London too. Leaving England for a haven of beach babes and movie dreams in The Golden State of California – a place without tears.

*

Dotting at her damp eyes Maggie could feel the damage her earlier fall had caused her – the bruises mottling her skin and swelling her features. She did not feel like walking any further and instead hobbled over the stones to the forecourt of the nearest boozer. She passed through the crowd of rebel smokers clustered around heaters on the streets, as tramps would an oil drum fire, and entered the comforting haven of the pub. Maggie had always managed to find a semblance of solace in the babblings of the beer-drinking masses. It became her sanctuary, her quiet among everyone else's noise. She scanned the room. This was one of the few remaining 'proper pubs', the kind that members of the Campaign for Real Ale would worship and take yearly coach trip pilgrimages to. The name was etched into frosted window glass that prevented people seeing in or out. The surface of the solid, dark wooden furniture was scuffed with glass rings and pre-ban cigarette burns, while the occasional chair sat lop-sided from a former bar brawl injury or three. Booths were draped in red velvet, worn threadbare by hundreds of passing arses. The fabric wore dark stains where a hen night girl had vomited or an angry lover had poured a pint over her partner.

At 3 p.m. it was pretty much deserted and Pink Floyd was blaring through the tinny speakers. A woman who turned out to be the landlady was singing along, sliding off her stool at the bar, while in her right hand sloshed a large chardonnay. The orange lipstick she coated her lips and teeth with also wrapped itself around the glass. Her skirt was short and her hair long and pulled up in a girlish high ponytail giving her a cheap face lift. She was forty going on sixteen. Her childish blue eyes bulged, rolling back into her head like a doll's.

'Yes, love,' she sang in Maggie's direction, but didn't move to pour her the drink. Instead a tall, wiry young man stooped on the right side of the bar to hear Maggie order a large glass of house red without slurring – she was well practised in the art of appearing sober when she was not. His slightly greasy straight hair hung to his shirt collar. As he placed the tipple down before her, dwarfed between his unexpectedly elegant fingers, the landlady fell off her stool without spilling a drop of her drink. Maggie started forward to help her up, but nobody else did. The woman swayed back to her feet all by herself, saying to the barman: 'I'll be going back upstairs now, if you need me.' She grabbed another bottle from the fridge and departed, knocking debris flying as she went.

'Not likely,' the barman muttered. He was relieved; he knew that would be the last he would see of his boss today. As he waited patiently for Maggie to pick a late lunch option off the menu and count out the money for her wine and the food he turned down the music and surveyed the pub. Most of the usual back bar crowd were out on AA pub crawls, or irritating their horrible families, or sleeping off the previous day's excesses.

The money machines – loudly broadcasting their terrible, bleepy dance music – were situated in the corner by the gents, which Maggie could smell all the way from the bar. The pub, now smoke-free for five months (if you didn't count the after hours chain-smoking lock-ins for staff and regulars), stank. No longer cloaked in the foggy stench of tobacco stale and new, it now reeked of blocked urinals, stagnating dregs' buckets and drunks' farts and body odour, while everything looked too clean, outlines too defined. Maggie, who had preferred the reassuring cover of smog, craned her head this way and that, seeking out one of the worst lit corners in which to drown her sorrows and numb her aches and pains.

The barman thanked Maggie warmly. He was not wary of her type of customer – the unhinged, the alcoholic, the lost, or the lonely. The pub, somewhere the misfits of society could feel welcome, needed more patrons like Maggie to counteract the newcomers. The smoking ban had brought an unbearable kind of clientele back into the bar – those superior than thou women and worse, their children who ripped up beer mats and knocked over the inebriated.

Maggie smiled back at the barman and took her numbered wooden spoon and her glass of wine over to a table as far as possible from the stench of the gents. Settling in a worn red velvet armchair her thoughts returned to her recent broken affair with Simon and, as always, to Allan. Her one true love. Old conversations cascaded and his face was replaced by shards of memories and fragmented features and she'd plummet, freefalling through them, wrapped in the fading scent of him. Of all the men since Allan, and there had been plenty, few had got under her skin, and none had won her over as he had. They were welcome distractions and partial obsessions but they were far from being her air for breathing, her *raison d'être*. Amy knew better. Her friends knew better. Maggie deep down had an inkling of this too: why else was she still smarting from Simon's recent exit from her life? 'The two-faced sod,' she muttered as her glass emptied in one blushing gulp.

She had met Simon in a bar. Not the run-down establishments she often frequented these days, but a pristine new place that had opened up near her office. She'd gone in for a quiet drink after work with one of her clients – a short busty woman called Dawn. They had worked together for years, but this was a social call. A light bite to eat, two glasses of wine, and then home. Maggie had been insistent on these terms. She had curbed her drinking at the time after a scare – she had nearly set the house on fire when Amy was asleep. The small flames had sobered her up quickly, hurled her into action and all that suffered were a couple of tea towels and her grill pan, but she had discovered that her smoke alarm was faulty. It had shocked her into better behaviour. She was on top of things at work and getting on with Amy most of the time. She was bright-eyed with possibility again. When Dawn had disappeared off to the ladies for the umpteenth time, Simon had caught Maggie's eye from the bar. When Dawn returned he had asked if he could buy them a drink, join them for a while. Dawn had winked at Maggie, and she had been right to. Simon was far more appealing than any of the dates she'd had that year. He had taken her number before she left and called the next day. He had turned out to be quick-witted and knowledgeable with a firecracker of a sense of humour. It wasn't long before their meetings became more regular and involved a lot less clothes.

Maggie had spotted the white band of skin from a missing wedding ring the first time they had met, when he had drummed his fingers on the table as he perused the menu or considered an answer to one of her questions. It hadn't deterred her. He wouldn't have been the first man she had dated who had technically belonged to somebody else. If she was honest, many of the men since Allan had been the same. As such, Simon's wife hadn't been a problem for Maggie initially. She hadn't even figured in her mind, let alone invoked jealousy or pangs of guilt. Instead Maggie had dived into the relationship, lapping up the gifts and the attention. The clandestine meetings, the good restaurants. As with her other affairs Maggie had felt herself growing dependent upon Simon, perhaps due to her increasing age and that of her daughter; Amy would soon be old enough to leave home. Maggie's fear of being alone for life felt more possible by the day. It wasn't just that, though: everything about this relationship had felt different for Maggie. It was the closest anything had come to her good times with Allan. She wanted to know where he was every minute of the day and she had eventually grown jealous of his wife and children. She abhorred anybody who kept Simon from spending time with her. She recognised the neurosis from all those years before and she was petrified. Maggie wanted Simon all to herself, she was so afraid of another rejection, of him leaving her like Allan before him, and yet it was inevitable. The more she manipulated the situation in an attempt to regain control, the more Simon began to despise her. He was plotting a way to leave her without sabotaging his marriage or invoking her suicide.

By the night of their ruined dinner, their last encounter, Maggie had fallen for him. Well and truly. She was close to breaking point, too close to calling his home and announcing the affair to the other legally bound woman. It had to stop. Simon's wife was everything Maggie despised in a woman, not simply because she was married to him. A petite and delicate English rose, better suited to his business-meets-pleasure dinner parties. A woman hailing from good moneyed stock. Maggie saw red when she thought of her, the anger so intense it scared her. She wasn't normally one for horror stories but the sickest ideas flashed through her mind at that moment. She was glad to know she wasn't even in the same city as Simon and his wife then. She was no threat to anyone in her seaside pub.

Maggie wasn't an English rose, she was Welsh for starters, and she was strange-looking, alien. It was said that she had been unusually beautiful in her youth, but now middle age was being unkind. She winced at her reflection in the huge pub mirror on the wall facing her, shocked at the old, now partially swollen doll face staring back; the heavy crows' feet clawing at her glassy eyes. She still felt twenty-three inside, but had become more and more aware of her own mortality as the body expressed its aches and pains, its limits reached. She seemed to age simply by watching her reflection, noticing each new wrinkle and grey hair; wiry and held stubbornly erect.

'You're not that old, Mum,' Amy would joke, seeing her mother frowning at the mirror when getting ready for a date.

'Just you wait...' Maggie would shoot back, for a second despising her daughter's youthful exuberance and smooth, creaseless face beaming beneath Allan's curls. She was her father's daughter alright. It drove her to distraction. The two of them shared more traits than seemed fair to Maggie. She would look at Amy and feel such an intense mix of love and hate. This creature that she adored more than anything in the world, who so resembled the person she despised most. The nose, the facial expressions, the humour and the curls. It was uncanny. The girl had barely spent any time with the man, and yet she still had his mannerisms, his scathingly dry wit. It was no wonder Maggie and Amy fought. As the initial shock of Amy's photograph had dissipated, she pulled it out to examine it again. Maggie fingered the paper printout. He wasn't a patch on Simon, she laughed, surprising herself. There was a time when she had so wanted to be Allan's wife. Tracing the outline of his body, she noticed how and where he had sagged and extended, and how differently the pair of them had aged. How far from grace he had fallen. Maggie had more wrinkles but less weight. She was still angry, but more than that she was afraid for Amy and the fallout of this, of all she had been through in the past six months. It was a lot for a teenager, for anyone to handle. Cremating your lover and then meeting your father after seventeen odd years. She had always pushed for things, wanting more just like her father, and, thinking of that feisty spirit Maggie had when working in the chip shop and setting the fringe theatres of London ablaze, like her mother too. When Amy had told Maggie about her plans to go travelling she had done exactly that: *told* her. It wasn't a debate, it was a done deal. While Maggie had pleaded with Allan not to go to America she didn't even try to change Amy's mind. She knew it would only have served to send her further and for longer. She wanted Amy to do things differently to her father; she wanted her to come back.

*

Maggie leant back in her seat, noticing a newspaper tucked under the table. She flicked through the stories to the TV guide, which revealed another night of sport highlights and cooking shows. The pub seemed to be getting rowdier now, conversations that had initially been so hushed she had not detected them were now turning up the volume – laughter and swearing loudly punctuating the bubbles of chatter. Usually a comforting noise for Maggie, the volume instead made her want to retreat. Looking around, she didn't feel the usual loose connection, the unspoken camaraderie she had come to expect from the bar. The place had filled up. Expensively dressed students drinking top price drinks – all bought on their loan account – gathered clumsily by the bar watching the door. Solo drinkers, mostly male, perched around the room, half an eye on the horse racing on the telly. One old soak sat on a stool by the back bar, caked in make-up, her brass-coloured top revealing a push-up bra, one wrinkled tit shrivelling inside each purple satin cup. Maggie didn't want to end up like her. She didn't want the students to see them both and assume they were one and the same. She drank a lot when she was down, she self-medicated her moods or escaped them in a haze of vin rouge, but most of the time she was completely functional.

Maggie was also not as alone as she sometimes let herself think – she had a good circle of friends, it's just that they were all women, and all middle-aged women at that. If they hadn't settled down then they basically hibernated through the winter, settling their bloated backsides into the sofa cushions and eating their Marks & Spencer's meals for one in front of whatever reality TV they'd block recorded on Sky Plus – *Big Brother*, *America's Next Top Model*, *X Factor*, *Strictly Come Dancing* or *I'm a Celebrity Get Me Out of Here*. She'd tried to get them to leave the house before, but she knew better these days. When the sun started shining it would be easier. They'd be back at the gym and their aqua aerobics classes, which meant chances to nab them for drinks afterwards. Later they'd be taking their slightly less wobbly bodies to community carnival workshops, ready for the various street festivals where they'd be belly-dancing their hearts out for a chance of Jamaican cock.

The friends of hers that had married or settled down were equally terrible to visit when you were single or going through a rocky patch. It wasn't that they were smug, far from it. They were often claiming to be jealous of Maggie's life, of her freedom to pick and choose. It was that even when they were complaining about all their partner's faults she was jealous of them – regardless of how the men didn't pick up after themselves or how they always got a takeaway if it was their turn to cook. How they spent hours with their geeky and childish hobbies, didn't make any effort with their appearance. How rarely they had sex, and how mechanical it was, how quickly it was over, how unattractive this made them feel. Maggie knew all this, but she also knew that those friends would not be sat in a pub alone, paranoid that people were looking at her, pointing at the sad woman with the bruised chin drinking on her own, and making their mental notes not to turn out like her.

Suddenly, home seemed more appealing.

*

Back in London a scent lingered on the platform, sweet and cloying like treacle – the remnants of a gaggle of teenage giggles. Maggie surfaced to street level in the blue half-light where birds squawked and swooped about her like bats. She had drunk herself sober, or to some semblance of it. She felt ruined, shattered, and ready to sleep long and deep. It was a feeling she hadn't had for a while. She traipsed along the high street over discarded newspapers, broken umbrellas and half eaten kebabs. She staggered past barber shops and internet cafés, off-licences and world food stores, signs offering international phone cards. She stopped by one and considered calling Amy, but remembered she didn't have a number for her, and besides she couldn't work out the time difference. Amy would probably be asleep or out exploring anyway. Maggie homed in on her destination, the terraced road virtually deserted, the street lights guiding her in to land, counting them down to her doorstep, her house.

Arriving indoors Maggie shrugged off her coat and boots and made her way slowly through the house to the bedroom, turning the heating up and the lights off. She stopped by the computer, still glowing and humming from the night before. She had e-mails: some from work, a few from a theatre director whose calls she was still ignoring – for how much longer? – and one from Amy.

Maggie shut down the PC without reading Amy's words.

They could wait until tomorrow.

She had waited so long to hear what had become of her first big love, a few more hours wouldn't hurt. She climbed the stairs and curled up, fully clothed, under the bed sheets – drifting deep into dreamland under a quilted blanket of stars.

Above her, planes arrived and departed, taking weary travellers to the people and places they did and did not want to see.

Acknowledgements

Versions of some of these stories have been previously printed elsewhere. 'Pica' has featured on www.theraconteur.co.uk and 'Diving Lessons' appeared in the 2009 Parthian anthology *Nu: fiction & stuff*.

Thanks, thanks and more thanks. Firstly to Lucy, Dom and Rich at Parthian, but especially Lucy, Queen Editor, top friend. Massive thanks to the diamond Seattle poet Graham Isaac (to whom I owe much, including a broken toe). Thanks also to all those who have read and/or encouraged versions of these works, other scribbles and myself, namely: Stevie Davies, Nigel Jenkins, Fflur Dafydd, Angela Phillips, fellow students on the MA in Creative Writing at Swansea University (2006–2008), Clare Sherratt, Bethany Sullivan, Julianya Jay, Clancy Hood, The Crunch, Carys Kelly, Sophia Davies, Rose Pearl, John Williams, Tristan Hughes, Niall Griffiths, Matthew David Scott, Aneurin Gareth Thomas, Lloyd Robson, Peter Wilson, *The Raconteur*, Boys From The Hill, Tim Wells, Matt Whyman, EEF, *Mslexia*, *Buzz*, Adam Sillman, Tom Green, Chris Mason, Tim Prosser, Tomos Owen, Francesca Rhydderch, Academi, Honno, Mab and Mao Jones, Lucy Narramore, and last but not (quite) least – THANK YOU Useless.

I also owe bucket loads of glittered gratitude to caffeine, real ale and those people and places that have fed, accommodated or entertained me in times of true poetic or romantic impoverishment; or bought me drinks. Shiny happy stars go to the White family, the Bristol massive, Rachel Trezise, Huw Rees, Eleanor Thorne and Jim Bailey, Jonathan Powell, Kate Gething-Lewis, Claire Easterman, Jonathan Anderson, Undercurrents, The Chattery, Elysium Gallery, Kirsten Harvey, Samuel Linthorne, Nick Dosanjh, Liam

Shaolin Wolf, Ray Boothby, Jarrad Young, Rosy Cait Steel, Rhiannon Morgan, Richard Jones, Mozart's, The Brunswick, Team Kruger, Emily Byrne, Mark Valentine, guitars and rock stars, The Dylan Thomas Centre (cheers Jo, Al and Dave), Sera Rabbett, Wynne Davies, Antonio Carra, The Rags, Boatbar, Karma Junkie and KoD, Swansea Central Library, and many a creative, eccentric, drunk or free spirit in the Uplands Triangle and beyond.